Darkness Exposed

A MARY O'REILLY PARANORMAL MYSTERY

by

Terri Reid

The night is darkening round me,
The wild winds coldly blow;
But a tyrant spell has bound me
And I cannot, cannot go.

~Emily Bronte

This book is to all those who face darkness and defeat it every day. May we remember that darkness can only be conquered with light and hate can only be overcome with love.

DARKNESS EXPOSED – A MARY O'REILLY
PARANORMAL MYSTERY

by

Terri Reid

Copyright © 2011 by Terri Reid

The author would like to thank those who
have contributed in the creation of this book. The
editors: Ruth Ann Mulnix, Jan Hinds and Debbie
Deutsch. The invaluable assistant: Sarah Reid. The
medical consultants: Dr. Craig Johnson and Martha
Johnson, PT. And the patient husband: Richard Reid.
Thank you all!

Prologue

Sycamore, Illinois – 8 years ago

Jeannine Alden wiped the counter in the kitchen for the fourth time. She bit down on her lower lip, glanced at the clock and then looked longingly at the staircase to the second floor. Really, she was only five months pregnant, she wasn't an invalid. She could probably paint the whole room before Bradley even got home from work. She could open the windows so the fumes wouldn't be too bad.

She could already imagine Bradley's arguments. *What if you fell off the ladder? What if you strained yourself opening the windows? What if the fumes were worse than you thought?* What if? What if? What if?

She quickly sat down on a stool next to the breakfast bar and got a kick in her rib for the effort. Grinning, she rubbed her hand gently against her swollen abdomen. "Oh, so you want to have a say in the matter too?" she cooed to her unborn child.

Her unborn daughter. They were going to have a baby girl.

Sighing, she remembered the look on Bradley's face as they watched their daughter move on the ultrasound's screen. She smiled as he stared, awestruck, at the little squirming body. He looked down at her, tears filling his eyes, and placed his hand on her belly. "She's beautiful," he said, "just like her mother."

She sighed again. *How could you not love a man who said things like that?*

Glancing up the stairs again, she slumped back against the stool. And as soon as he said those lovely words, the awe was replaced by a fierce protectiveness. "You need to take care of yourself," he said. "I don't want you doing any heavy housework or any lifting. I'll take care of that."

She remembered the radiologist grinning behind Bradley's back and winking at Jeannine. Yes, she knew she would eventually get around his over-protective attitude, but it wouldn't be the day after the ultrasound. So, painting the nursery was going to have to wait.

A tall glass of icy lemonade sat at the end of the counter. She had poured it and another when one of her neighbors had dropped by for a quick visit. She wondered if Bradley had put him up to it, just to be sure she wasn't overdoing it. She wouldn't put it past him. Reaching for the glass, she drank deeply. Pregnancy made her so thirsty. But then, of course, she knew soon she would have to rush to the bathroom. It seemed to be a never-ending cycle – liquid in, liquid out.

The thought of the going to the bathroom seemed to signal to her bladder, so she slid off the stool and started toward the hall when a knock on the back door stopped her. She turned and saw another neighbor, Mercedes Wasserman, peering through the break in the door's white cotton café curtains. "Jeannine, Jeannine, are you home?"

Groaning inwardly, Jeannine turned back to the door. Mercedes was the worst gossip in the community and never had a nice thing to say about anyone. She sincerely hoped Bradley hadn't enlisted Mercedes's help in checking on her throughout the day. She would probably end up saying something rude to her and it would end up all over the neighborhood. She pressed the buttons to disarm the alarm, grabbed the doorknob, she schooled her face into a pleasant expression and opened the door.

"Mercedes, how nice to see you," she lied pleasantly.

Mercedes leaned forward and pecked on each of Jeannine's cheeks. "Darling, don't you just look radiant," she gushed. "Pregnancy certainly agrees with you."

"Thank you," Jeannine replied. "I'd love to ask you in, but…"

Mercedes slipped past her into the kitchen and placed a Longaberger basket draped in a red gingham check on the counter. "I actually baked for you," she said, her voice raising an octave to an annoying trill, "wholesome, whole-grain blueberry muffins. Yum."

She unveiled them, took one out and handed it Jeannine. "You know how important it is for you to get your daily requirements of fiber," she coaxed. "Go on, try it."

Jeannine politely took the pastry, silently noting that it weighed much more than she would have guessed. She hefted it in her hand. "Wow, that's solid."

Mercedes nodded. "Oh, yes, I used whole wheat, wheat bran and psyllium," she said. "You're not going to get any more fiber than that."

"Have you tried them?" Jeannine asked hesitantly.

Mercedes shook her head. "Oh, no, darling, I could never eat something so bulky with my petite figure. But with all that extra weight you've put on, no one would even notice a couple muffins."

She giggled. "Darling, you could eat a dozen!"

"Really, Mercedes, don't hold back on my account," Jeannine said.

"Oh, I didn't mean it that way," she quickly recanted. "I mean, well, it looks good on you. Really! I wish I could carry weight like you do."

"Thanks, Mercedes," Jeannine replied, wondering if she would leave a mark if she whipped the muffin at Mercedes. "But, really, I just ate."

"Oh, no, you have to at least try it," Mercedes said, hopping onto one of the barstools. "I'm not leaving until you do."

Jeannine immediately bit into the unappetizing muffin and just as quickly regretted it. The rough and dry texture was combined with an overly sweet taste. She chewed slowly, praying she could swallow and keep it down.

"Oh, do you like?"

Jeannine pasted a pleasant smile on her face, nodded, and continued to chew.

"I'm slightly jealous of you," Mercedes admitted. "I've always wanted a baby, but for some reason, I can't get pregnant."

She leaned closer. "Although, truth be told, I'm sure it's Harvey's fault," she said with a shrug. "He's just not...well, you know...well loaded. But I'm sure your Bradley is..."

Jeannine choked and Mercedes passed her the unfinished glass of lemonade.

"I should have warned you that you should only eat them with a drink close by."

Jeannine nodded her head and silently decided the kind of drink that would make these muffins palatable was not on her list of approved beverages while she was pregnant. She sipped on the lemonade and winced, the tart taste intensified by the sugariness of the pastry. Finally, she closed her eyes and swallowed, praying it all stayed down.

"Thank you, Mercedes, that was so...refreshing," she said, "and very thoughtful of you."

But when Jeannine looked up, Mercedes seemed to be swimming in front of her. Jeannine grabbed the side of the counter, hoping for the wave of dizziness to pass.

"My dear, are you all right?" Mercedes's voice seemed to come from far away. "You look positively green."

Jeannine thought she detected a pleased note in Mercedes's voice. "I'm fine," she said, taking a deep breath and willing the lightheadedness away. "It's just nap time. I must have overdone today. You'll have to excuse me, but if I don't take my nap, Bradley will be furious with me."

"Are you sure you don't want me to stay?" Mercedes asked. "I could make phone calls while you slept."

"No, no," Jeannine insisted, nearly pushing Mercedes out the door. "Really, I'll be fine."

Once the door was firmly closed behind Mercedes, Jeannine leaned her head against the wall. The dizziness was increasing. She felt like the floor was moving beneath her. Something was wrong; she had never felt like this before. She needed to call Bradley. She needed him to come home.

She remembered her phone was on the table next to the couch. Using the walls, counters and furniture for support, she slowly made her way to the living room. She collapsed onto the couch and reached for her phone. Bringing it to her, she realized she couldn't see the numbers clearly. She tried to dial anyway, but she couldn't bring her fingers to press the right buttons.

The room was starting to sway and she had to close her eyes to keep from getting sick. She laid down on the couch, her hands over her abdomen, tears streaming down her face. "Bradley," she called out weakly. "Bradley, come home, I need you."

# # # #

Owww, my head, Jeannine thought as she opened her eyes. *How long have I been asleep?* Her vision was still blurry and she felt exhausted. She didn't even have the strength to sit up. She slowly turned her head and couldn't see anything. *It must be nighttime. I must have slept into the night. But why didn't Bradley wake me up?*

"Bradley."

"I'm sorry, but Bradley won't be coming to help you."

The voice was coming from behind her, but it sounded slow and deep.

"Who are you? Why do you sound funny?"

She knew she should panic, but she couldn't seem to make her body react.

Soft laughter filled the room. "My voice is just fine, my dear. I would guess the drugs are having an effect on your hearing."

"Drugs? I can't be on drugs. The baby…" she said.

"Oh, don't worry about that," the voice responded. "I'm going to take very good care of you and the baby. We don't want the baby to be hurt. We want a nice healthy baby."

"But…Bradley. I want to see Bradley."

She heard the scuffle of feet across the room. She sensed a body standing over her, but her vision was too blurred for her to see who it was. She felt her shirt being lifted, her stomach exposed to the cold, damp air that surrounded her and then felt a hand slowly caress her abdomen. She shivered and tried to recoil, but her body wouldn't move.

"Please," she pleaded. "Don't hurt my baby."

"Oh, darling, I don't want to hurt your baby," the voice replied, as the hand continued to stroke her skin. "I love the baby. I love *our baby*."

Chapter One

Mary O'Reilly awoke with a start. Someone was banging on her front door at the unheard hour of…she glanced at the clock on her bed stand. *Nine o'clock! Crap! It's already nine o'clock?*

Mary was a former Chicago police officer who had been shot in the line of duty several years ago. She actually died on the operating table and started her final journey down a long tunnel toward a light. Before she reached the light a voice called out her name and gave her a choice. She could continue to the light, or she could go back to her life and her family, but things would be different. She chose to return and soon found the promised change was the ability to see and communicate with ghosts. After recovering from the surgery, she decided to move to the small town of Freeport, Illinois, open a private investigation agency and solve cases involving ghosts.

Sliding out of the covers, Mary grabbed her robe and headed down the stairs. Then she remembered her house guest, Professor Ian MacDougal from the University of Edinburgh. Ian was researching paranormal activity and law enforcement. Mary's brother, Sean, had asked her to allow Ian to work with her for a few weeks. But because of bad weather and airport delays, Ian hadn't arrived until two o'clock in the morning; Mary prayed the noise didn't wake him.

"Can Mary come outside and play?"

Mary grinned when she heard the familiar voice of her ten-year-old neighbor, Andy Brennan.

"Well, I dinna ken. She stayed up 'til the wee hours of the morning and might need to be resting awhile yet."

Mary recognized Ian's voice too. She stopped and leaned back on the wall, blatantly eavesdropping on the conversation.

"You talk funny," Andy replied. "Are you a foreigner or something?"

"Aye, I'm from the wilds of Scotland."

"No! Honest? Scotland?" Andy asked. "Is that by where Harry Potter lives?"

"Oh, yes, it is," Ian replied. "I live not more than two hours north of Hogwarts School."

"But Hogwarts isn't real, it's just a book."

"Yes, but Alnwick Castle in Northumberland, where they filmed the movie, is very real. And it's near the border of Scotland."

"You live near a castle?"

"There are over 250 castles in Scotland."

"Wow! Do you live in a castle?"

"Well, now I'm living in a flat, but last year I lived in Edinburgh Castle doing research on some of their ghosts."

"Mary, I mean, Miss O'Reilly, has ghosts," Andy said. "She helps them. My mom says she's a blessed lady with a special gift. But, Mrs. Hawes, down the street, she says Mary's a nutcase."

Ian chuckled. "And what do you think?" he asked.

"I think she's great," Andy said. "And she's much more fun than a normal grown-up."

"I bet she is," he said. "And, if I'm not mistaken, our Mary is up and listening as we blether on here."

Laughing as she descended the stairs, she got a good look at Ian in the daylight. He certainly did not look like any professor she had in college. If he had, she would have stayed to get her PhD, at the very least. He was built like he spent quite a bit of time in the gym, but he had the sun-bleached hair and tanned skin of a man who was very familiar with being in the outdoors. That morning he was dressed in loose sweatpants that hung low on his hips, a gray t-shirt with "Real Men Wear Kilts" plastered on the back and one of her white baker's aprons over his front.

"Hey, Mary, I really like your Scot guy," Andy said. "Even though he talks funny."

Andy was dressed like an Eskimo, his bright blue eyes shining beneath his wool cap.

"We'll just have to teach him how to speak properly," Mary said, and then she sniffed the air. "Did you make breakfast?"

"Aye, I was thinking I'd have to serve it to you in your bed," Ian replied.

"I only get to eat in bed when I'm sick," Andy said. "Mary, are you sick today?"

Mary came over, pulled the wool cap off his head and ruffled his red hair. "Do I look sick to you?" she asked.

He breathed an audible sigh of relief. "Good, 'cause if you was sick, I'd be in real trouble."

Ian looked back and forth between the two. "And you'd be in trouble because?"

Andy shrugged. "Well, a bad guy got Mary and she was in the hospital, then she came home and the police chief told her she had to rest. But, instead she went sledding with me and my brothers yesterday."

Ian looked at Mary. "You went sledding?"

"Shhh, it's a secret," she said. "And nothing happened. I'm just fine. Right, Andy?"

Andy grinned. "Right."

"So, did you make enough breakfast for Andy too?" she asked. "Although I must warn you, he has two hollow legs that can hold four dozen doughnuts."

Andy laughed. "And eight brownies."

Mary nodded. "And four milkshakes."

"And two hundred French fries," Andy giggled.

"Well, I might have made just enough, then," Ian said. "Why don't you come in and see."

They walked together into the kitchen and Mary looked at the food he'd already prepared. There was plate of eggs, another of toast, a large bowl of oatmeal and about a pound of bacon was on the

12

griddle. "Were you expecting company?" she asked. "A lot of company?"

Looking a little embarrassed, he glanced over at the food. "So, Yanks don't start the day with a hearty breakfast as they mention on the television?" he asked.

"What have you been watching, The Waltons?" she asked.

He grinned. "Aye, I was a wee bit sad when you dinna yell good night to me."

Laughing, she picked up two of the platters and carried them to the table. "Well, I hope both of you men are hungry."

Andy threw off his coat and scooted onto a chair at the table. "I sure am."

Ian carried the bowl of oatmeal and the bacon to the table and sat next to Andy. "Would you have some porridge?" he asked, offering him the oatmeal.

"Really, this is porridge?" he asked, looking at the thick pasty brown substance. "It kind of looks like oatmeal."

Grinning, he scooped a portion out and plopped it into a smaller bowl. "It is oatmeal," he said, "Scottish oatmeal."

Mary watched Andy glance around the table, looking for something. "What do you need?"

"Brown sugar and raisins," he replied, "for the oatmeal."

"You're not going to be ruining a good pot of porridge with sugar, are you?"

"Ruining it?" Andy asked Ian.

"Aye," he said. "All you need is a bit of salt and a spoon."

"Salt?" Mary asked, wrinkling her nose. "Salt? That's disgusting."

"It's traditional," he argued, folding his arms across his chest.

"Scots people eat weird food," Andy said solemnly.

"We do not," Ian argued.

Mary got up and got the brown sugar and raisins from the cupboard. "Well, you do eat haggis," she said.

"What's haggis?" Andy asked.

Ian looked stunned. "You don't like haggis?"

Mary handed the items to Andy and sat down. Then she leaned forward toward him and said, "Haggis is sheep stomach."

"Gross," he said, as he liberally sprinkled brown sugar on his porridge. "Do you really eat that?"

Ian leaned over toward Andy. "Aye, but only to gross out my brothers," he said.

"Cool," Andy replied. "Can we make some?"

Laughing, Ian patted Andy on the shoulder. "Aye, I think we need to make a big batch so we can share."

Twenty minutes later, after Andy had eaten more food than both Mary and Ian, he looked at the clock and sighed. "I s'pose I need to go home now, Mom said I wasn't to make a nuisance of myself," he said.

"Well, you can tell your mom that you weren't at all a nuisance, you were a great help," Mary said. "How could we have eaten all that oatmeal if not for you?"

"Mary, it wasn't oatmeal, it was porridge," he corrected her.

"Aye, Mary it was porridge," Ian added.

"Well then, you tell your mother that you ate genuine Scottish porridge for breakfast," Mary added, helping Andy button up his coat.

"Can you come out later or do you have to take care of Ian?"

Mary chuckled. "Perhaps we could invite Ian to come out too."

Andy turned to him. "Ian, do you want to come out and play?"

"Well, I wouldna mind a walk in the fresh air," he confessed. "I was cooped up in an airplane all day and my lungs are crying for fresh air."

"Do you ice skate?" Andy asked.

"Aye, but I dinna think to bring mine along."

"Oh, no problem," Mary said. "I keep extra pairs of skates here for when my brothers visit. I'm sure we'll find a pair that will fit you."

"Then I'll be joining you, Andy my lad," he said.

"Okay, great," Andy said rushing to the door. "I'll tell my brothers. We'll be back in a little bit, okay? I'll tell them you lived in a castle. This will be so cool."

Andy hurried out the door and pulled it closed behind him.

"He's quite a lad," Ian said. "Wears you out just watching him."

"I know," Mary laughed. "If I had half his energy, I'd be happy."

Mary stood, stacked the dishes on top of each other and started to move to the sink, when Ian stood up and blocked the way. He took the dishes from her hands, placed them back on the table and put his hands on her shoulders.

"Tell me about the hospital," he said. "And the bad guy Andy spoke of. Are you in danger?"

"I was working on a case last week," she said. "And I got in a tussle with the bad guy. Really, it was no big deal."

"Yeah, no big deal if you're into electric shock treatment," Mike said, appearing next to Mary.

Ian, who was also able to see ghosts, jumped. But Mary was far too used to this behavior to react.

Mike Richards, a former fireman, was now a ghost. He and Mary met while she was investigating a serial killer who poisoned men who didn't return her affections. Mike had been one of her victims. But now Mike was a bit of an enigma. Generally, when a case was solved, the ghosts were able to move on to the next life. But, for some reason, Mike didn't move on. Instead, he became Mary's friend and confidant.

"Mike," Ian choked, hoping his heart would settle back to a regular beat. "Do you always just appear like that?"

Mike shrugged. "Yeah, it's pretty much how I do it," he said. "I figured if only my head showed up it might freak Mary out."

"I can understand that," Ian said. "Now, tell me about the electric shock treatment."

"I got some bruises, a couple of scrapes and some burns," she said. "The doctors released me from the hospital. I'm fine. Really."

"Should you be going skating?" he asked.

She put her hands on her hips and stared defiantly at him. "Try and stop me," she said.

Ian looked her over, stood up and picked up the dishes. "I'm a far wiser man than that, Mary O'Reilly."

Chapter Two

Thirty minutes later, Andy, his two older brothers, Colin and Derik, and his eight-year-old sister, Maggie, were at the front door, ready to escort them to the park. Mary almost didn't notice the freezing temperatures as they walked down the street. Ian kept them all entertained with his stories about ghostly encounters in Scotland. She was pretty sure she didn't want to visit the underground city of Edinburgh. His stories about the apparitions and spirits that inhabited those dark caverns made her blood run cold.

"So, I dinna understand," Ian said, as the children ran ahead to put on their skates. "You deal with ghosts every day, and yet, you dinna want to come tour the underground city with me."

"I help ghosts who need to have a problem solved or something finished up before they can move on," she explained. "They are just regular people who died in a way that has left them waiting for someone to tie up their loose ends. They aren't malevolent spirits who want to hurt people; they are usually just confused, frightened, sad or lonely. Sometimes they don't even realize they're dead."

"Ah, so you're not working with scary specters and ghoulies that go bump in the night," he said, nodding his head in understanding, "but lost souls looking for peace."

She nodded, "Yes, that's it exactly. I don't want to deal with demons or evil spirits; I don't have those kinds of skills. I just want to help those sent to me."

"But you believe there are those kind – the evil ones – about us?"

Considering her answer for a moment, she waited before she finally spoke. "I've seen too many people – living people – who do such terrible things that I can't deny it. Evil is out there and it's strong. But I know that good is stronger. So that's where I put my efforts."

"You're an amazing lass, Mary O'Reilly," he said.

She smiled. "Wait until you see me on ice skates."

Less than ten minutes later, Mary was extending her hand to Ian and being pulled out of her third snow drift of the morning.

"Well, I wouldna believed it, had you warned me," Ian said with a smirk. "You are truly amazing on the ice. The likes of which I've truly never seen before in me life."

Mary dusted herself off. "This time it wasn't my fault," she protested. "There was a bump in the ice."

He nodded. "Ah, yes, I see it there," he said, looking over to the slight rise in the ice. "Truly 'tis a hazard. Someone should place a warning light near it."

"You're mocking me, aren't you?" she asked.

He grinned. "Oh, no, not I? I wouldna dare."

She shook her head. "Keep it up and I'll make haggis for dinner tonight."

"Mary! Mary! I mean Miss O'Reilly," Andy called as he skated up to her. "I saw you skate. That was awesome."

Mary smirked at Ian. "Thank you, Andy."

"You did that on purpose, right?" he asked.

Ian coughed loudly into his glove and Mary glared at him.

"Well," she began and then sighed, knowing she had to be honest with him. "No, I didn't, I tripped on the bump in the ice."

"What bump?" Andy demanded, looking around the area.

"That one, over there," Mary pointed out the offending ridge.

"Gosh, Miss O'Reilly, that's really not much of a…" Andy stopped once Ian had sent him a meaningful look. "I mean, that would have made me fall too, for sure."

Mary shook her head. "Andy, what has your mother told you about lying?"

"Well, if it's for a good cause, like telling someone they look good even if they look like a jerk, it's okay. So, good skating Miss O'Reilly."

This time Ian didn't even bother to cover the laughter.

"Thanks, Andy. Thanks a lot!"

"Sure, anytime," he grinned. "So, want to play crack the whip with us?"

"Crack the whip?" Mary asked. "Only if I get to be on the end."

"Oh, no," Ian said. "You've just recently come from the hospital. You'll be doing harm to yourself."

"I've played crack the whip since I was a baby," she said. "I have never once slipped off the end of the line."

"I really don't like this idea," Ian said.

"Come on," Mary laughed. "It'll be fun."

They joined a group of eight other skaters, Ian in the front and Mary at the end. They began to circle the rink, slowly gaining speed and momentum. Mary felt the wind brush against her face and breathed in the cold, crisp pine-scented air. She was holding hands with Maggie, who was chuckling delightedly as they spun in a giant round. Mary laughed at sheer joy of the sound.

Suddenly, Colin started to move past Ian and change directions of the line. Mary could feel the whole line react with a sharp jerk. Ian sped up, trying to regain the head, but Colin took it as a challenge and jerked the line in the opposite direction.

Mary looked down at Maggie whose face had changed from delight to trepidation. Her little gloved hand was beginning to slip out of her brother's hand on the other side. Mary knew she only had one choice.

"Maggie, I'm going to let go," she said. "Then you grab Andy's arm with both of your hands to be safe. Okay?"

Maggie nodded slowly. Mary took a deep breath and let go just as the line cracked again. Her first thought was amazement at the sheer speed she was traveling toward the large drifts of snow on the other side of the rink. Her second thought, before she headed toward the inevitable crash once again was, "Well crap!"

Chapter Three

Freeport Police Chief Bradley Alden popped open the can of Diet Pepsi and drank deeply, hoping the caffeine would kick start his system. He hadn't slept well the night before. During the early part of the evening he had dreamt about Mary O'Reilly and had finally realized through the dream she hadn't lied to him about his wife, Jeannine.

Jeannine had been missing for over eight years, after a break-in at their home in Sycamore, Illinois. Bradley had spent the better part of that time searching across the United States for any clue that would lead him to his wife. He didn't know if she was dead or alive, or if she had been taken or had chosen to run away from him and his job as a police officer. Finally, when he had run out of money and realized he was no closer to the truth than he had been eight years ago, he applied for the job in Freeport and tried to pick up the pieces of his shattered life.

And that's when he met Mary O'Reilly.

Tossing the now empty can into the trash can, he pulled a second from the fridge. *Mary O'Reilly,* he thought, *he should have run away when he first met her.*

He had actually met Mary before he knew who she was. They both had a habit of running at the park early in the morning. They ended up with an unspoken competition, racing each other through the park and then separating at the conclusion, neither uttering a sound. He had heard rumors at the office about the crazy psychic who thought she could see and hear ghosts. He already had the woman pictured in his mind; a middle-aged, caftan-wearing, earth mother with a copious number of pendants and crystals resting on her ample bosom. But when Stanley, the owner of Wagner's Office Products, had introduced him to Mary and he realized she was the mystery woman from the park, he was stunned.

In the next few months, as she proved not only her competence and courage, but also the truth about her ability to communicate with ghosts, Bradley found himself admiring the professional and falling in love with the woman.

He looked at the toppled chair on the kitchen floor. He remembered whipping his jacket at it when he got home from his middle-of-the-night drive to Mary's. He walked over, picked up his jacket, set the chair aright and sat in it, cradling his head in his hands. "What the hell was I thinking?" he muttered.

When he had woken from the first dream and realized that he had unfairly judged Mary, he donned jeans, his jacket and a pair of house slippers and had driven over to her house. If his car had not been parked in the garage, he might have remembered the snow and ice storm. Once there he was definitely reminded about it as he slid and scrambled his way up and across Mary's porch. He finally made it to

Mary's door only to have it opened by a strange man with a Scottish accent, looking quite at home. He could recall the conversation perfectly.

"Where's Mary?" he had asked.

The stranger paused for a moment and then met his eyes. "She's upstairs, getting ready for bed," he said.

Bradley felt a hit to his solar plexus.

"Getting ready for bed," he repeated, "with you here?"

Smiling widely, the man nodded, "Aye, I was just on my way upstairs when I heard you on the porch."

"But, she's getting ready for bed," he repeated, trying to make sense out of the statement.

"Aye, it's been a long day. I dinnae think she was expecting you, we were both looking forward to bed."

"You were both," he choked on his words, "both looking forward to bed?"

"Aye. Would you bide a moment whilst I fetch her?" he had asked, nodding his head in the direction of the stairs.

Bradley had shaken his head. "No," he said. "It seems that it was later than I thought. Much, much later."

He had turned and slowly slid across the deck to the post.

"Could I tell her who called?" the man had called after him.

"No one," Bradley had replied, grasping the banister and climbing slowly down the stairs. "No one at all."

Bradley lifted his head slowly and his eye caught sight of one of his slippers lying on the top of the fireplace mantel. He remembered throwing them across the room too. He walked across the room. There, next to the errant slipper, was a dried and brittle piece of mistletoe. Picking it up, he twirled it in his fingers, one lone white berry still attached to the stem. It had been a gift to him from the ghost of a young boy he and Mary had helped during the holidays. Hanging above them in Mary's kitchen, it had given him the motivation he needed to pull Mary into his arms and finally tell her how he felt. He could still see her looking up at him, her eyes filled with love and wonder.

Another vision flashed across his mind, a vision that had haunted his dreams for the remainder of the night and had left him frustrated and angry. Mary in someone else's arms, laughing, smiling and looking up at someone else with those same eyes filled with love. His Mary. Lost. And he had no one to blame but himself.

He started to tighten his hand into a fist, but felt the delicate leaves begin to crumble and carefully placed the mistletoe back on the mantel. The final white berry dislodged and rolled across the slick surface. Catching it before it fell to the floor, he held it in his hand for a moment and finally dropped it into the shirt pocket of his uniform, next to his heart. No matter what, he would always cherish the time they spent together.

He looked at the other object on the mantel; a silver framed photo of Jeannine and him on their wedding day. He picked up the photo and looked into her eyes.

She was happy, he thought, *and we loved each other.*

Breathing a heavy sigh of remorse, he shook his head and whispered, "Jeannine, I'm so sorry I failed you. And now I've failed Mary too."

"You weren't always such an idiot."

Bradley spun around to see Jeannine's translucent form hovering across the room. Her arms were crossed over her chest and her face was set with determination.

"I need your help right now," she said. "And, really, standing around feeling sorry for yourself isn't going to solve my murder. So pull yourself together, okay?"

Bradley was speechless for a moment.

"What do you mean, feeling sorry for myself?" he finally blurted out. "My heart is broken here."

"Oh, well, maybe if you hadn't treated Mary like she was a liar, hadn't acted like a jerk while you asked for her help and basically threw her love back in her face, you wouldn't be in the situation you are in right now," she said.

"But, but, but," he sputtered. "I told her I loved her."

Jeannine sighed loudly. "Bradley, love is more than just words. Love is action. Words are easy, backing them up every day with what you do and what you say is when you really prove what you feel."

"I loved you," he said.

She smiled sadly. "Yes, you did," she said. "And I knew it because you were willing to change to save our marriage. You fought for me, Bradley. Fight for Mary."

He shook his head. "She's got a new guy," he said. "And he's got an accent."

Jeannine grinned and she shook her head slightly. "So what, you've got a sexy uniform," she countered. "Uniforms always ace out accents. Besides, she loves you and that trumps all."

"Really?" he asked. "Still? Even after all I've done?"

"Go find out," she said.

Chapter Four

When Bradley left a few minutes later he absently switched off the lights and closed the door firmly behind him. Jeannine, alone in the living room, was left standing in the dark. The sound of the door closing and the darkness triggered a flutter in the pit of her stomach. She started to fade away, then stopped.

What if the panic has something to do with my murder? she thought.

Although she couldn't remember much about her death, she realized she hadn't even thought about it until she found Bradley in Chicago a few months ago. Before then she had been floating helplessly between this life and the next trying to find resolution.

Forcing herself to remain calm, she tried to think back and remember why she would be afraid of the dark. She closed her eyes and searched her memory.

"Darling, I'm home."

The voice seemed to echo in the small chamber. Jeannine breathed in the gust of fresh air, then the door closed and once again the stale, damp air of the room surrounded her.

"Have you been a good girl today? I brought you a present. But first, your medicine."

29

She shook her head, "No. No drugs," her voice came out hoarse and dry.

She felt the hand on her jaw and the metal cup pressed against her lips. She tried to shake her head, but she was never strong enough. She gagged as the liquid was forced down her throat. "There, there, my dear, it's not all that bad."

She tried to fight it, tried to fight the drug and the power it had over her mind and her will. "I hate you," she whispered, tears streaming down her cheeks.

She felt lips press against her temple. "Ah, yes, my dear, but in a few moments, you will love me once again."

She shook her head. "No, never."

"But, darling, you don't remember do you? You don't remember what you do when your medicine takes control."

She felt the hand move past her shirt and stroke her bare skin. "I make you very happy, Jeannine. You cry out to me in ecstasy."

"No!" she cried, her voice slurring. "No, I don't want you."

"Oh, darling, you want me. You've always wanted me. You just needed me to free you from the clutches of your husband. It was always me. And this baby has always been ours."

She shook her head, trying to clear the fog from her brain. "No, this is my baby. This is Bradley's baby."

The fog was thicker. She couldn't think, couldn't remember. She felt the hands again, stroking, moving over her body.

"You like this, don't you darling?"

"Please," she whispered, a final tear threading its way down her cheek.

"Oh, yes, darling, you please me very much indeed."

Jeannine shook with revulsion as she came back to the present. She didn't have a better idea of who had done this to her, but at least she understood why she couldn't remember the details of her death. She had been drugged.

She needed to let Mary know what she'd remembered and Bradley would have to know too. She shuddered again.

But first she needed to think things through before she shared them with anyone.

Chapter Five

Bradley found himself heading to Mary's house once again. He was going to fight for her! *Well, at least I'm going to talk to her*, he thought, *and give that Scottish Casanova a thing or two to think about.*

He turned right and headed down Empire Avenue toward Mary's home. As he drove past the park a familiar figure caught his eye. He slowed the cruiser down and stared. It couldn't be Mary out on the ice, could it?

He pulled on to the emergency lane that ran through the park and headed toward the rink. *Damn, that is Mary!*

Parking the cruiser on the side of the lane, he jumped out and started to jog toward the rink. His jog broke into a run when he saw her slip from the chain and race toward the edge of the rink.

"Well, crap," Mary thought, as she hurtled toward a very large pile of ice covered snow. "This is definitely going to hurt."

She closed her eyes and braced for the impact. "Oomph."

That was not a snowdrift, she thought, as strong arms closed around her and shielded her from the impact. *It must be Ian.*

"Wow, you skated to the rescue…" she stopped midsentence once her eyes were fully open and she realized it was Bradley holding her in his arms. They were both lying on top of a four-foot pile of snow. "Bradley!"

He raised one eyebrow. "You were expecting someone else?"

"Um, no," she stuttered. "I was…it was…a…surprise. That's all."

Bending her head away from him, she couldn't believe how intensely guilty she felt being caught participating in outdoor activities. She had promised him she would take it easy all weekend.

Bradley could see the guilt spread across her face. *Damn, that can only mean one thing. She slept with that Scottish Cassanova.*

Ian and Andy brought their skates to a quick stop when they saw Bradley help Mary. Andy shook his head. "She's in trouble now. Can a grown-up get grounded?"

Ian grinned. "Well, I guess we're going to find out. Shall we wait and see if she needs our help?"

"Yeah, but let's watch from this far away," Andy replied. "I don't want the police chief to get mad at me. It was my idea we go sledding."

"That's a cunning plan, Andy," Ian agreed.

Bradley held Mary loosely in his arms. "Are you hurt?"

Shaking her head, she looked up into his eyes and smiled. "No, I'm not," she said. "Thanks. How about you? Are you okay?"

He started to respond, but then he stopped. "I need to be honest with you and I hope you can be honest with me."

"Of course," she said. "I'll be honest with you."

After taking a deep breath, he met her eyes directly. "I know about yesterday."

Crap, how did he find out about the sledding? she wondered.

"I'm sorry," she said. "I know I promised, but really, I was so bored."

"You did it because you were bored?" he asked incredulously.

"Well, that, and he was pretty hard to resist," she said with a smile. "He really does know how to wheedle his way into my heart."

Bradley's heart sunk. He realized he had been hoping it had been a misunderstanding. That she hadn't slept with him.

"But, Mary, after all you said about waiting," he insisted.

"I know," she admitted. "And I really had planned to wait. But I really didn't see the harm in it. Although, to be honest, I was really exhausted afterwards."

"Well, that's the usual outcome," he replied bitterly.

"I probably would have been okay if I had stopped after an hour," she said. "But after three hours, I could barely lift my legs."

"Three hours?" he gasped. "Mary, that's impossible."

"I know, right?" she replied. "I couldn't believe it either. We'd just finish and then it was time to start up all over again. I mean it was fun; actually, it was pretty exhilarating. But all that work for just a few moments of excitement and, poof, then it's over."

"But you enjoyed yourself?" he asked. "I know it was your first time."

Mary was confused. "First time?" she asked. "Bradley, I grew up in Chicago. I've done it hundreds of time. But I haven't really taken the time to do it lately."

"But I thought you said…"

"Thank heavens his mother called and interrupted us," Mary continued. "They would have had to pull me home on the sled. And let me tell you, only my pride prevented me from begging for a ride anyway."

Bradley shook his head to clear it. "Mary, what are we talking about?" he asked.

"Sledding with Andy Brennan and his brothers on Saturday," she said. "Right?"

Ian watched the conversation between the two and saw the confused look in Bradley's eyes. *What in the world are they discussing?* He decided it was time to skate over and reintroduce himself.

35

"Andy, me lad, I'm going over to help our Mary," he said. "It looks like things could be getting a little fierce."

Andy looked up at Ian. "Do you think I should come too?" he asked. "I mean I was the one who made her go."

Ian chuckled. "No, but I'll be sure to let the chief know you are willing to take the fall for Mary."

Andy smiled. "Thanks, Ian."

Andy skated back to his siblings and Ian skated to Mary and Bradley.

"Morning, Constable," he said, skating to a halt next to them. "Looks like you saved the day."

Mary turned to Ian. "You know Bradley?"

"Oh, aye, we met last night whilst you were making up my bed," he replied easily. "But he left in a hurry and I dinna get the chance to introduce myself."

Mary turned back to Bradley. "You came to my house last night?" she asked. "Why didn't you stay?"

She had been honest with him; he had to be honest with her. "I thought I was interrupting something."

"Interrupting?" she repeated.

At first she was confused, then she thought back to the conversation they'd been having before Ian introduced himself. "That's what we were just talking about, wasn't it?"

She pushed herself out of his arms, stumbled, and would have fallen if Ian hadn't caught her. But

36

she was oblivious to all of it. She was only aware of the boiling anger and hurt raging through her body.

"You thought that I...that Ian and I...after all I said," she said, closing her eyes a moment to try and control her feelings. "I had hoped you thought better of me."

The single tear that slid down her cheek broke his heart. "Mary, I'm sorry," he said. "But what was I supposed to think when I come to your house in the middle of the night and a man answers your door?"

"You were supposed to trust me," she said, "which really has been the issue between us for quite a while."

She angrily wiped the tear away from her face. "I have to go now, Bradley," she said. "I don't want to talk with you anymore."

She turned away.

"But our meeting," he called after her.

She quickly whipped back to face him. "I gave you my word that I would help you with Jeannine's case," she said bitterly. "And although you don't find much value in it, my word is my bond."

She skated across the rink, leaving Ian and Bradley alone facing each other.

Bradley turned to Ian. "So, who the hell are you?"

Ian shrugged. "I'm a professor from the University of Edinburgh. I'm on a joint fellowship with the University of Chicago researching paranormal entities and criminalistic methodology."

Bradley lifted an eyebrow.

"Ghosts and solving crimes," Ian said. "Sean figured Mary would be the perfect person to help me with my work."

"Ah, so Sean sent you here," Bradley said, nodding his head. "And what did Sean tell you about me?"

"That you were a bloody idiot who was breaking his sister's heart."

"Well, he's right about the idiot part," Bradley agreed. "Have you ever been in love?"

"Oh, aye, Gillian, my fiancée back home who'd rip my heart out of my chest and serve it with jam if she'd thought I'd even looked at another woman," he said with a sigh. "I miss her terrible."

Bradley chuckled. "I should have known better, she wouldn't have slept with you."

"Aye. Her heart's already taken, I ken."

Bradley shrugged. "Well, it was," he agreed, "until I acted like a fool. I've got a lot to apologize for."

"Well, no time like the present, Constable," Ian said. "Would you be willing to give a man a ride home?"

Bradley nodded. "Let's take the long way, give her a chance to cool down."

"You might have to drive to Scotland for that."

"You're probably right."

Chapter Six

Mary slammed the door with all of her might. "The big jerk," she yelled, throwing her bag across the room.

Mike appeared behind her. "Okay, so now that the dead are awake," he said. "You wanna tell me what the trouble is?"

"Men are idiots," she said, pulling her coat off and angrily shoving it into the closet. "All men are idiots."

"Should I be offended, or are you just referring to living men?" he asked.

"Don't patronize me," she said, turning and glaring at him. "All men, living and or dead."

"Wow! So what did we do? I mean other than starting wars, destroying civilizations and being generally insensitive and smelly?"

Mary faced him, ready to fight, when a large tear escaped from her eye and ran down her cheek. She tried to sniff it back, but once the first one escaped, she had no control of the others.

"I really hate him," she cried, sitting down on the couch and burying her head in her hands.

"Well, of course you do," Mike said, floating over next to her. "What did the big, bad, police chief do this time?"

She looked up at him, her face tear-stained, and her nose runny. She grabbed a tissue from a nearby box and blew noisily. "How did you know it was Bradley?" she asked.

He looked at her for a moment and shook his head. "Tell me."

"He thought I slept with Ian."

"Well, where would he get an idea like that?" Mike asked, hoping she didn't find out about his part in the charade the night before.

"Well, I was skating and I was going to crash…"

"Of course you were," Mike interrupted, which earned him another glare.

"And Bradley happened to be there and he caught me."

"Well, that was romantic," Mike said. "Prince Charming rescuing the damsel in distress."

Mary sniffed again. "Then he told me he knew about yesterday."

"Yesterday? What happened yesterday?"

"Well, I thought he found out that I had gone sledding with the Brennan boys," she said. "But when I tried to explain, he thought I was talking about sleeping with Ian."

"No!" Mike asked incredulously.

"Yes," Mary replied. "And I have no idea how he could have mistaken anything I said for having sex."

Mike turned his head slightly away from Mary. "Mistaking sledding for sex? I don't see the connection either," he said, his voice slightly strained. "So, what did you say?"

"Well, first, I wanted him to understand that I didn't purposely break my promise to him, but I was so bored, so I agreed to do it," she said.

"Okay, you were bored," Mike repeated, "sounds innocent enough."

Mary paused, trying to remember how the conversation had progressed and listing the items sequentially. "I told him that it was really exhilarating, but I was exhausted afterwards. I told him that if we had just done it for an hour or so, I would have been fine, but after three hours I could barely lift my legs."

She turned to Mike. "You know, climbing that hill over and over again is exhausting!"

Mike just nodded.

"Then the last thing I said was that it was a lot of work for just a few moments of fun," she added. "How could he think I was talking about anything else but sledding?"

Mike was silent. Mary looked over at him. He had turned fully away from her, his shoulders were shaking, but he was completely silent. "Mike?"

He shook his head, but didn't turn back.

"Mike, are you okay?"

He nodded, but didn't turn around.

"Mike, what's wrong?"

Then she heard it, a small snort.

"Are you laughing at me?"

He shook his head, but his body shook even harder.

"You! You! Man!! You are laughing at me!" she cried, picking up the box of tissues and throwing them at him.

The box flew through him, but it got his attention and he turned to face her. "I'm sorry, darling, but…damn…that is the funniest thing I've heard in a long time."

"It's not…"

"Oh, come on now," he choked. "Three hours? Couldn't lift my legs? A lot of work for a few moments of fun? Darling, you have to see…"

Mary stopped and finally listened to what she'd said. She placed her hand over her mouth and her face turned beet red. "Oh my," she gasped.

"Could have been worse," Mike said.

"How?" Mary asked.

"Well, Bradley," he said, raising his voice to mimic hers. "Next time I'd like to try a bigger one, because really, the elevation on that one was pretty small."

He was laughing so hard he had slipped off the couch and was floating across the floor.

"Mike!" Mary said, turning even redder. "That's not funny."

Barely able to speak, he shook his head. "Oh, no, Mary, it's not just funny, it's hysterical."

"Stop it right now," she insisted.

He faded away.

"Good riddance to you," she yelled into the empty room.

A moment later, Mike reappeared in front of her with a devilish grin on his face. "You could have told him that you slid off and almost hurt yourself."

Mary gasped. "Get out! Now!"

With his laughter trailing behind him, Mike disappeared just as the door opened and Ian stepped inside.

"Mary, look who I've brought home with me."

Mary turned to see Bradley following Ian into her house.

Chapter Seven

Well, crap! I am so not in the mood for this.

"Um, Mary, I was wondering if I could come in?" Bradley asked.

"Why?" she snapped. "Is there something else you'd like to accuse me of?"

Ian moved in front of Bradley, as if to shield him and pulled his cap off his head. "I have a confession to make," Ian started. "Last night, when Bradley came to the door. I…"

Bradley quickly moved around Ian. "It wasn't his fault, I shouldn't have believed him," Bradley interrupted.

"It was my fault; I made him think that we'd…" Ian began.

"Wait a moment," Mary said, holding up her hands and halting their words. "I am really tired of all of this. Ian, what did you say to Bradley last night when he came to the door?"

"I told him you were upstairs getting ready for bed," he said, sheepishly. "That we were both looking forward to a good night's sleep."

"You didn't tell him that I was getting the guest bedroom ready for you?" she asked.

He shook his head and met her eyes straight on. "No, I didn't. I made it seem like we were cozying down together."

"And why would you do that?" she asked, the thread of an idea forming in her head. "As you had barely met me?"

Ian looked away quickly. "I've a nasty sense of humor and it seemed the thing to do at the time."

Mary didn't hesitate; she punched the speed-dial for her brother's cell phone and put it on speaker.

"Good morning, Mary," her brother, Sean, answered cheerfully. "And how are you this fine day?"

"Well, I'm in a bit of a pickle," she said sweetly. "It seems I'm a fallen woman now. Your friend Ian had his way with me last night."

"Why, the son of a…" Sean yelled. "He told me he was engaged to be married. He told me I'd have nothing to worry about. He was supposed to get your Bradley a little jealous, that's all."

Then the line went quiet for a moment. "Did he hurt you Mary?" he asked. "Are you okay?"

"Damn you, Sean O'Reilly," Mary said, wiping the tears out of her eyes, "for being both an interfering lout and a tender-hearted bastard. I'm fine, no thanks to you. And I'll have you know that Ian MacDougal did not lay a hand on me, but he was also not going to tell tales on the likes of you. So I had to trick you into a confession."

Once again, the line went silent for a moment. She heard a deep sigh.

"Mary, can you forgive me?" Sean asked.

"I'll think about it and let you know," she said, and disconnected the call.

Then she turned on Ian. "And I let you into my home," she said. "I gave you a bed, shared my food with you and you, nothing but a wolf in sheep's clothing."

"You're right," he replied, moving toward the staircase. "I'll pack my things and be out in a trice."

"Did I say I was going to throw you out?" she asked.

He stopped in his tracks. "No, but I thought…"

"I gave my word," she said, quickly glaring at Bradley, "not that it means much these days. But you can stay. However, if I find you meddling in my affairs again, I'll call your fiancée and let her know that you and I had fun making up the bed the other night."

"Aye, that's threat enough to put the fear of God in me," he said. "I do apologize, Mary. I truly meant you no harm."

She turned to Bradley. "Do you really have so little faith in me that you could believe one moment I would swear my love to you and the next I'd sleep with another man?"

"I thought I'd chased you away," he said simply. "I'd dreamt about you and in the dream I remembered that you hadn't lied about Jeannine. That you had told me all you could, all the way back on New Year's Day. I'd gotten out of bed and hurried here, to apologize. Then I met Ian at the door and thought I was too late. Can you forgive me?"

The same words Sean used, but it was so much harder to hear them coming from Bradley. She knew she'd forgive Sean. She'd done it hundreds of times in her life. But Bradley? He had such power to hurt her, to break her heart.

She closed her eyes against the tears. She was not going to cry. Bradley Alden was not going to make her cry again.

Taking a deep breath, she opened her eyes and faced him. She owed him at least the chance she'd given Sean. "Bradley, I'll think about it and let you know."

He nodded. "That's fair. Thank you. So, where do we go from here?"

"We move forward," she said. "And we work on solving Jeannine's case."

As if on cue, Jeannine appeared in the room across from Mary. Her face was streaked with tears and she was visibly trembling. "Mary, I remembered," she cried. "I remembered and it was awful."

Chapter Eight

There was complete silence in the room when Jeannine finished sharing her memory. Bradley sat on the recliner in the corner of the room, his elbows on his knees, his hands clasped tightly together and his head bowed. Mary could feel the tension in his body from across the room. She understood his anger and his frustration, as a cop she'd been very familiar with those feelings, especially when a good collar got away because of a technicality in court. A technicality that had more to do with an under-the-counter payment than bad police work.

But what she knew she could never truly understand was the underlying guilt Bradley was experiencing. Jeannine had been his wife; he was supposed to protect her and their unborn child. In his mind, he'd failed. And now, hearing how she'd been treated, it had to be eating him alive.

Okay, she'd given him a few minutes to brood, but now they had to put together a plan. "So, it's obvious this person knew both you and Bradley," Mary said. "And they had access to your home because you were taken from your house to this other place."

"I suppose," Jeannine said. "But why would one of our friends do something like this?"

Bradley suddenly stood and strode out of the room.

Jeannine turned to Mary. "He has to know he did everything he could," she said. "He searched for me for years."

"Yes, he did," Mary agreed. "But finding out that you were taken by a neighbor and were probably kept close by is making him second guess everything he did. Even if he did everything right."

"Would you talk to him?" she asked. "I think coming from a former police officer, he might actually listen."

Mary nodded. "Yeah, I'll be right back."

The backdoor was unlocked and when she looked through the window, she saw Bradley standing at the railing, staring up into the night's sky. She grabbed a coat from a hook and slipped out the door to join him.

The temperature was below freezing and Mary wondered if he even noticed. She stood next to Bradley and tried to follow his gaze upward. "That's Orion," she said.

He turned to her. "Excuse me?"

She pointed to the constellation above them. "Orion, the Hunter," she said. "That's him up there."

"How ironic," Bradley muttered, turning and leaning against the railing. "Too bad he wasn't available eight years ago."

"Were you the only one on the case eight years ago?" Mary asked.

"No, there was an official investigation, I wasn't allowed on that one," he said. "My chief felt I was too close."

"And they didn't find her either," she said. "Did they?"

"That doesn't matter, Mary," he said. "Did you hear what he did to her? Did you hear how he drugged her? How he touched her? And all because I didn't find her."

"Okay, listen, I can't crawl into your body and try to figure everything's that's going on in there," she said. "But I do know we have a fresh angle on a creep who killed eight years ago. For all we know he's still kidnapping women and subjecting them to the same torture Jeannine just told us about. So, I understand you feel like you let her down. I understand you're frustrated. But, right now, we've got to put together a plan to catch this guy so he never does it again and so Jeannine can finally be at peace."

Bradley closed his eyes and stood still in the cold night air. He finally took a deep breath and opened his eyes. Steely resolve filled his eyes, replacing the anger and self-contempt. "Okay, you're right. Let's go in and figure out how to catch this bastard."

They joined Ian and Jeannine in the front room. Mary slipped down next to the fireplace and Bradley sat back in the recliner on the edge of the room.

Jeannine moved across the room and sat on the floor, next to Bradley. "Are you okay?"

He nodded and turned to her. "I'm so sorry," he said. "I'm sorry I didn't find you and get you away from him."

"I know you tried to find me," she said, tears sliding down her translucent cheeks. "I know you did the best you could. I'm sorry I wasn't stronger. I thought about breaking out when the drugs were wearing off, but I was so afraid. I'm sorry, I kept thinking there would be a chance, but I guess it never came."

"You can't blame yourself," he said. "I'm sure you did everything you could."

She smiled at him. "Then you can't blame yourself," she repeated. "Because I know you did everything you could."

He sighed. "But you were so close, if I had only…"

"Stop it," she demanded. "Right now. No more thoughts of yesterday. It's done, Bradley. Now we have to move forward. Help me find him. Help me find who did this to me."

"I promise, I will find him," he said, and then he glanced over at Mary. "We will find him."

Mary couldn't hear what Jeannine and Bradley were discussing, but she liked the look of determination and resolve she saw on his face after the discussion had ended. *Good for you, Jeannine.*

"Okay, are we ready to talk about this?" she asked.

They all nodded their agreement.

"Good," Mary said. "Now obviously, Jeannine is the key to finding this guy. Her memories will bring us closer than anything else."

"Jeannine, what triggered your memories today?" Bradley asked.

"When you left the house, you turned off the lights and closed the door," she said. "That's what he would do. He'd leave me in the dark and close the door."

"I'm sorry," Bradley began, "I didn't think…"

"Don't be sorry," Jeannine said. "It helped."

"So, your memory was triggered by being in a similar circumstance," Mary said. "We could try other stimulus and see if it opens up more memories."

"Yes, but because she doesn't have a physical body anymore, we're limited by the kind of stimuli we can offer," Ian said. "It has to be more environmental and things that affect only two senses, hearing and sight. Unless I'm mistaken, you don't have the sense of smell, do you Jeannine?"

Jeannine laughed shortly. "Why no, I don't. I hadn't thought of it, but I can't smell anything."

"And can you feel heat or cold?"

She shook her head. "No, I can't."

"So, we have to be in an environment where sounds and sights can trigger her memories," Ian said. "There's something else. It's never been tried, but it may work."

"What's that?" Bradley asked.

"Hypnosis," Ian suggested. "It's often used to bring back hidden memories. But there's been cases where the subject remembers what was suggested to her, rather than what actually happened."

"What do you mean that it's never been tried?" Bradley asked.

Ian grinned. "Well, I can't be sure, but I'm betting hypnosis has never been tried on a ghost. I'm not sure how that would work. You wouldn't want her beaming out when she was in a trance."

"Do you know how to hypnotize someone?" Mary asked.

"Aye, I've done quite a bit of study in hypnosis, especially as I've studied psychic phenomena," Ian said. "They've found that hypnosis can actually aid in the occurrence of many forms of ESP, you ken, Extra Sensory Perception. Hypnotized persons tend to perform better in laboratory tests of clairvoyance, telepathy, and precognition."

Mary leaned back, letting the warmth of the fire heat her back, and studied Ian for a moment.

"So, Mary, you have a look in your eye that seems a bit dangerous," Ian said. "What is on the mind of Mary O'Reilly?"

She chuckled and nodded. "I'm wondering how much adventure you were looking for when you signed on to this fellowship?"

"Ahh, I see," Ian said. "You thought perhaps I was interested in reading your wee diaries, sipping on tea and chewing a scone in my study, eh? And here, you offer me a chance to work with a ghost, solve a murder and apprehend a serial killer? Aye, I'll leave the scones and sign up for the adventure. Tell me what you'd have me do."

"You're a good man, Ian MacDougal," Mary said. "And perhaps we can throw in some scones on the way. Bradley, I have an idea. But, I want you to listen to me before you make a decision."

"That doesn't sound like a promising beginning," Bradley said, then he sighed. "Okay, I'm listening."

"First, do you know who owns your old house?" Mary asked.

Bradley nodded. "Yeah, I do," he said. "I never sold it. I always thought that if Jeannine decided to come back, she'd want to…"

His voice broke and he looked down at the floor.

Jeannine turned and looked up at him. "That was lovely," she said. "I always loved that house. Thank you for saving it for me."

He nodded, but didn't trust his voice yet.

"Okay, well, that makes this plan even easier," Mary said. "First, hypnosis always works better in familiar surroundings, so not only would it be better for Jeannine to be there for the hypnosis, something else around the house might trigger other memories. We also know that whoever did this was either a neighbor or a friend, someone Jeannine would let into her home, right?"

Mary looked around the room, ensuring everyone was on the same page, because the next part was going to be the hard one to get agreement on.

"We also know that some of the neighbors were hesitant to say anything to Bradley because they believed that Jeannine was having an affair."

"Which was completely untrue," Jeannine inserted.

Mary nodded. "Yes, completely untrue," she agreed. "But somehow the rumor got started and because of it, Bradley didn't get the information he needed to find Jeannine. So, it would be interesting to find out how those rumors got started and who the neighbors thought the mystery man was. The information they held closely eight years ago might be the very thing to unlock the mystery today."

"But why would they talk to me now?" Bradley asked.

"They probably won't," Mary said. "Because they either believe that Jeannine ran away with the other man, or they feel guilty they didn't tell you the truth in the first place."

"So what good is my house?"

"Well, the nice thing about friendly neighbors is that they are usually all too willing to share tidbits of new information with new move-ins," Mary said and then took a deep breath before blurting out the next sentence. "Ian and I will pose as a couple renting your place. I'm sure just the fact that your house is occupied again will cause a stir in the neighborhood."

Bradley stood up. "Are you crazy?" he asked. "Do you think I'm going to let you become fresh bait for a killer?"

Mary stood too and faced Bradley from across the room. She kept her voice calm and low. "No, I think you will treat me like the professional law enforcement officer you know I am," she said, "and that you will have confidence in my abilities to investigate a murder and interrogate witnesses."

"And Ian?" Bradley asked. "Why is Ian the choice for your partner?"

"Because, quite frankly, you'd scare everyone away," she replied. "And because Ian can not only hypnotize Jeannine, he can also see ghosts. So, if this friendly neighbor is also a serial killer, Ian can help me locate any other lost souls."

Bradley ran his hand through his hair. "I don't like this," he said. "I don't like this one damn bit."

"I know," Mary said. "I know it's going to be hard for you, because you're going to have to be the behind-the-scenes person. And you're going to have to trust me."

He froze in his steps, then turned and met her eyes. "This has nothing to do with trust."

She met his eyes, unblinking. "This has everything to do with trust."

"May I just interject here?" Ian asked, breaking the tension in the room.

Bradley turned his glare on Ian. "What?"

"Although I don't have the years of experience you have in law enforcement, I have trained with Scotland Yard and I'm quite proficient in martial arts," he explained.

"How proficient?" Bradley asked.

"Sandan Black Belt," Ian responded.

"Third level," Bradley said, nodding with approval. "So, you're about as good as Mary."

Ian's eyes widened. "Well, it looks like I'll not have to worry about my safety either," he said with a grin.

Bradley cleared his throat. "Back to the matter at hand. Mary, how soon would you want to start?"

"How soon can you have the house ready for occupation?" she asked.

"Give me a day to make arrangements. How about Tuesday?"

"Okay, let's start Tuesday, if that's fine with you, Ian."

"Aye, I'm game," he said. "I've some gear that was going to be shipped here, if you'll give me the address, I'll have it shipped there."

Jeannine smiled. "This sounds like it's going to work."

Mary nodded. "Yes, Jeannine, I think it will."

Chapter Nine

"Why in tarnation was I asked to get here at the butt-crack of dawn, when no one seems to care if I'm here or not?" Stanley Wagner asked, standing in the front doorway of Mary's house Tuesday morning.

"Stanley, you're letting all of Mary's heat out," Rosie Pettigrew said. "Do come in and shut the door behind you."

Stanley grumbled to himself and moved inside, closing the door with a bang. "There, are you happy now?"

Rosie smiled sweetly. "Why, yes I am Stanley, thank you for asking."

Stanley rolled his eyes and walked through the living room and stood alongside the staircase. "Mary, you come down and explain yourself," he called up the stairs.

Stanley Wagner was the fifth generation owner of Wagner Office Supplies in downtown Freeport. And although the sixth generation was now running the store, Stanley still arrived early every day to greet the customers and make sure his children, now in their forties and fifties, were doing an acceptable job. He and Mary had become good friends when she moved to Freeport and now he considered her to be his responsibility, no matter what she said to the contrary.

"Stanley?" Mary called. "Is that you?"

"Darn tootin' it's me, missy," he said, pulling up on the waistband of his trousers. "And let me tell you, you've got some explaining to do."

"Now Stanley," Rosie said, moving around him to stand at the base of the stairs. "Mary is a grown woman; she doesn't really have to explain her actions to anyone."

Rosie Pettigrew was a successful real estate broker in her early sixties who also worked in downtown Freeport. She had been through about as many husbands as careers, and had been enjoying a flirty single life until just recently. Somehow Stanley's curmudgeonly personality snuck its way into her heart and her silly, prattling ways had done the same to his. But they were both desperately trying to ignore their new feelings, for fear if they acted on them they would destroy the friendship they both cherished.

Just then Ian jogged down the stairs, his arms filled with several suitcases. "Do you ken why women need ten times more clothes then men for the same time away?" he asked Stanley and Rosie.

Rosie looked at Ian and sighed. "And sometimes it's completely obvious why a woman would choose to do some things."

Stanley scooted around Rosie to block Ian's way. "And where do you think you're taking those suitcases?" he asked, his hands on his hips.

Ian stopped in his tracks and tilted his head in confusion. "Why, to the boot of the car," he said.

"The rental car, not the Roadster. I understand I'd be taking me own life in me hands to let her drive."

"I heard that," Mary called down the stairs.

"Auch, now you've done it," Ian said with a grin. "Here we are, not married for more than a day and I'm already in the doghouse."

"You're married?" Rosie gasped.

"Why would I be carrying her suitcases out of the house if we weren't?" he replied.

"Young lady, you come down these stairs now," Stanley called. "Or I'm coming up after you."

Mary quickly jogged down the stairs, a pair of shoes in each hand. "Rosie, if you can only bring a few pairs of shoes, because some people from foreign countries who shall remain nameless don't understand fashion, which would you choose? Heels or flats?"

"Well, darling, flats are more convenient, but heels are sexier," Rosie replied.

"She's bringing flats," Bradley called from the open front door.

Mary smiled. "Guess that answers that," she said. "I'm bringing heels."

"Would someone mind telling me what's going on and why I was asked to come here?" Stanley shouted above the clamor.

Mary paused on her way back up the stairs. "Oh, you were asked to come by?" she asked.

Rosie nodded. "Yes, Bradley called us up last night and asked us to come by this morning," she said. "Mary, I had no idea you had gotten married. I would have thought that you would have at least invited us to the ceremony."

Mary looked over their heads at Bradley who was standing behind them. "Would you care to explain to them?" she asked. "Since you did invite them to come over."

Bradley tugged at his collar for a moment and then looked at the two senior citizens. "Well, Mary and Ian are not really married," he said. "They are posing as a married couple to help me investigate a crime."

"Oh, well then," Rosie said. "I understand why we weren't invited. That's quite alright, Mary dear. I'm sure there's different etiquette involved when the weddings aren't real."

"There was no wedding," Stanley explained. "This is all pretend. It's a farce."

Rosie looked over at Ian and then back at Mary. "Really, this is all pretend?" she asked.

"We're just playing house," Ian said with a wink.

Rosie giggled. "If I were Mary, I think I'd prefer playing Post Office with you."

Ian looked confused and Mary laughed. "It's an American kissing game," she explained.

"Ah, we call it Spin the Bottle," he said.

"Oh, we play that game too," Rosie said.

"And how many different kissing games do you play here in the States?" Ian asked.

"Could we just get back to the business at hand?" Bradley asked.

"Of course, dear," Rosie said. "Ian, I can tell you about more kissing games later."

Bradley groaned. "The reason I asked Rosie and Stanley to come over is because I want them to aid in this investigation," Bradley announced. "I want them to go undercover with you."

There was a moment of silence and then the room was filled with an uproar of conversation.

"Really, dear, I don't think both Mary and I could both be married to Ian," Rosie said. "I think that's against the law."

"Rosie can't go undercover," Stanley shouted. "It's too dangerous. What are you thinking Alden?"

"Statistically speaking, the more people you bring in, the more likely the cover will be blown," Ian said.

"Well, I don't give a damn about statistics," Stanley countered. "I know that I can keep a secret."

"Oh, begging your pardon," Ian replied. "I didn't mean you couldn't."

Mary leaned against the railing and ignored the noise; she looked directly at Bradley, a question in her eyes. He shrugged a little sheepishly and shook his head. She tossed her head, indicating behind her, turned and quietly walked back up the stairs to her bedroom. A moment later Bradley joined her, closing the door and shutting out the noise from downstairs.

Mary turned, folded her arms across her chest and leaned back against the wall. "Well?"

He sighed. "I thought if Rosie and Stanley posed as your visiting grandparents it would be safer."

"You weren't worried about Ian and me sharing the house?"

He shook his head, his eyes widening in understanding. "Oh, well, of course you would have thought that," he said. "I haven't been exactly trusting lately, have I?"

Mary nodded slightly, not saying a word.

He moved toward her. "I'm sorry," he said. "No, I'm not worried about you and Ian. I'm worried about you. Mary, I…"

He stopped and turned his head to the side for a moment.

Mary could see he was struggling to control his emotions.

"Bradley?"

He turned back, his eyes determined and his gaze pointed. "Mary, this killer you are going after came into my house and took my wife, in broad daylight. He has been able to evade police for over eight years. He was cruel and he was sick. And now, now I'm supposed to send you into those same conditions and hope, no, pray that we are smarter this time?"

He turned away from her, ran his hand through his hair and finally turned back again. "I can't lose you too," he whispered, his voice breaking.

Although outwardly she looked calm, Mary's heart was pounding. After he found out about

Jeannine, Mary was sure her relationship with Bradley had been altered. Love doesn't grow where there isn't trust. Love couldn't grow when someone thought they'd been deceived.

Sighing, she shook her head. He just needed reassurance that he wasn't putting her in a dangerous situation without her full knowledge of the circumstance, she reasoned. He just needed to realize that she and Ian could do this.

"I know this is not easy for you," she said. "I know you want to protect me, us, because that's who you are and that's what you do. But this time, you can't. This time, the only way to catch this killer is for you to stay in the background."

"I know," he said, slowing moving toward her. "But what you don't seem to understand is this is not just about protecting you."

She shook her head and he could see that she really didn't comprehend what he'd been trying to say. He stopped in front of her, cupped her face in his hands and stared into her eyes. "You are my heart, Mary O'Reilly," he whispered. "I can't live without you."

He bent his head and placed soft kisses on her forehead, eyelids and along her jawline. The sweetness of the gesture and the tenderness of the kisses undid her. She trembled in his arms. "Bradley," she moaned, sliding her arms over his shoulders and threading her fingers through his hair.

He gathered her up in his arms. "Sweet, sweet Mary," he said hoarsely and bent his head to crush her lips in a heart-stealing kiss.

The world disappeared. All she was aware of was Bradley – his touch, his scent and the strength of his arms around her. She wanted the kiss to last forever. She moved even closer, pouring her heart into her response. He held her tighter, deepening the kiss. But after a few minutes, she felt his arms loosen as he slowly lifted his lips from hers.

"I know you need time," he said, breathlessly. "I'm not going to press you."

He stared down at her face, memorizing her swollen lips, her love-glazed eyes and flushed skin. Placing a final soft kiss on her lips, he stepped away, his hands sliding down her arms to her hands.

He lifted her hand to his lips, turned it and pressed a lingering kiss to her palm. "I love you," he whispered. "I know I've been a number one jackass lately, but I never stopped loving you."

He didn't give her a chance to respond; he simply released her hands, turned and let himself out of the room.

Mary slid down to the carpet and just stared at the closed door, running a hand over her swollen lips.

"Well, damn, girl," Mike said, appearing next to her. "If your heart isn't melting like chocolate in the sunshine, you aren't human."

"Shut up, Mike," Mary said, still staring at the door.

"What a man," Mike said.

Mary closed her eyes, nodded and sighed. "Oh, yeah, what a man."

Chapter Ten

"And so, when Bradley heard Earl walking back down the stairs and saw no one, and then the basement door opened and closed by itself, what did the poor man do?" Ian asked, as he changed lanes on Highway 39 on their way to Sycamore.

Mary laughed as she recalled the first time Bradley had seen a ghost in her home. "He finally let his gun fall to his side and told me there were no such things as ghosts."

Ian chuckled. "And what did you say to that?"

She shrugged. "I said, 'Oh, I keep forgetting' and then told him I was going back to bed and he could clean up the cookie jar."

"Ach, the poor, poor man," Ian said, without a shred of sympathy in his voice. "I remember the first time me poor fiancée, Gillian, spied a ghost. I was staying at Edinburgh Castle, doing research. It was into the evening and she thought she'd surprise me with a bit of supper. She was walking down one of the halls, almost to my room, and passed a lady who was dressed in late 17th century clothing. At first she just thought it was one of the guides, but after she passed, she realized that she could see through the lady. She felt a cold chill up her spine and turned quickly, but there was no one else in the hall now."

"Oh, poor Gillian," Mary said. "I'm sure she was frightened."

"Aye, our ghosties in Scotland tend to be a bit more gruesome than those here in the States," he said. "On closer reflection, Gillian recalled the woman had a darkening around her neck, where she'd been hanged."

"That sounds terrible."

"No, actually, it was quite nice," Ian admitted with a grin. "She had a bit more respect for the daft work she'd always thought I'd done and she was quite adamant about staying very close to me for the remainder of the night. I owe that bonnie ghostie a boon I'll never be able to repay. We became engaged on that very night."

"I so love a happy ending," Mary said.

Ian sighed. "Aye, so do I."

The GPS reminded them to exit and within ten minutes they found themselves pulling into the driveway of Bradley's home. Waiting on the front porch was a large assortment of boxes in varying shapes and sizes.

"Oh, good, they've arrived," Ian said, as he exited the car.

"What is all that?" Mary asked, looking at the pile of at least twenty boxes.

"Well, half of the boxes contain equipment I use when I study paranormal activity," he explained, as they pulled several suitcases out of the back of the car. "The other half is filled with my exercise equipment."

"You sent your exercise equipment all the way from Scotland?" she asked.

"Oh, no, I actually found a company in Chicago that would rent equipment while I was here," he said. "And since the delivery was made by the University, it wasn't a problem to have them bring it here, rather than Freeport."

Mary pulled the key from her purse and unlocked the door.

"So, what kind of equipment?" she asked.

"Well, mostly free weights," he said.

"Are you willing to share?"

He laughed. "Aye, I'd be happy to let you at them too."

It took them about an hour to unload the car and then to carry Ian's equipment into the house. Mary finally closed the door and leaned back against it, puffing from exertion, "That was harder than a workout," she panted.

"Aye," Ian agreed, resting his hands on his knees. "I told you not to bring so many clothes."

"Funny," she replied, wiping her brow with her sleeve. "What's next?"

"I think the next best step is to set up some of the equipment," Ian suggested.

"You want to exercise now?"

"No, the other equipment," Ian said. "I've cameras and infrared detectors that can not only pick up ghosts, but also any other kind of intruder we may encounter over the next little while."

"Well, that's brilliant," Mary said. "How many cameras do you have?"

"Well, enough for Edinburgh Castle, so more than enough to place all around this house," he said. "They're wireless, so we just have to set them up and route them to our network."

"So, we can access them from our laptops?"

"And I can send a link to Bradley," he said with a grin. "So, while he's lying awake at night, worrying about you, he'll have something to watch."

"That'll ease his mind a little."

"Aye, but only a little."

They worked together, setting up cameras throughout the house. Nearly every square inch was covered, except the bathrooms. Mary insisted she have at least a little privacy there. "There is no way someone will make it past all of these other cameras and only been seen in the bathroom," she argued. "Besides, I'm going to already feel like big brother is watching all the time."

"Oh, so Sean's told you he's to have a link in here too?" Ian teased.

She shook her head. "No, but I'm not surprised. When am I not going to be the baby sister?"

"Never," Ian said simply. "And it has nothing to do with your ability to take care of yourself and everything to do with their need to protect you."

Mary climbed down from the ladder she'd been perched upon and put her tools in Ian's toolbox. "I know," she sighed. "Men!"

Ian laughed and tried to sigh as fully. "Women!"

He walked over to his laptop and tested the cameras. "All fully functional and reporting," he said. "Now what's the next step?"

Mary picked up one of the boxes and started toward the kitchen. "I'll start getting the kitchen put together and you call for pizza," she said.

"That's a cunning plan," Ian said. "But why even get the kitchen put together? I'm fine with take-out."

Mary shot him a look over her shoulder. "Because Rosie and Stanley are coming tomorrow and Rosie cooks like a virtuoso."

"Ahhh, I wonder if she can make haggis?" Ian joked.

"Don't tease her about it," Mary warned, "because she'll take you seriously and we will be eating haggis for the rest of the time we're here."

Ian lifted his hands in surrender. "Thanks for the warning," he said. "I'll not be bringing it up."

Several hours later, with the house mostly put in order and the empty pizza box in the trash, Mary and Ian sat at the dining room table connected to Bradley via video chat.

"Any visitors today?" he asked.

Mary shook her head. "No, no one stopped by, which was probably a good thing because we got the cameras up and the house put in order."

"I hope they're just giving you a day to get settled," Bradley said. "The neighborhood tends to be quieter in the winter. People are not out and about as much."

"Do you have a list of people you'd like us to speak with?" Ian asked. "Anyone you've always had a feeling about, but could never confirm it?"

"I've been thinking about that," he said. "I'll e-mail you both the list and a little background on each of the families."

"Do you want us to touch base with your old Chief of Police, now that we're here?" Mary asked.

Bradley shook his head. "No, because whoever did this knew me and Jeannine," he said. "I hate to think that is was one of the guys on the force, but we can't be sure."

"It's tough having to consider everyone a suspect," Mary said.

"Yeah," he said. "But make sure you do. I don't want you to take any chances."

At that moment, the doorbell rang and Ian got up to answer the door.

"I'm not sure who that is yet," Mary said, "but I'm going to turn the laptop so whoever it is doesn't know you're chatting with us, okay?"

"Good idea," Bradley responded.

"I'll mute the sound too," she said, "in case your phone rings."

She made the adjustments just as Ian came back in the room, leading a tall man with dark hair that was graying on the edges.

"Mary, darling, this is Gary Copper," Ian said. "Actually, Dr. Gary Copper, a dentist and a friend of Bradley and Jeannine."

Mary quickly got up from the table and met him halfway, so he wouldn't see the computer screen. "Gary Copper?" Mary asked with a little smile.

The man smiled and bowed his head nervously. "Yeah, I know, not Gary Cooper," he said, and then he flushed. "Well, I guess you know that I'm not, well, you know. I'm not…"

"Gary Cooper," Mary finished for him.

He face turned red. "Yeah, that."

Mary smiled and extended her hand. "Well, it's nice to meet you Dr. Copper."

He took hold of her fingers and squeezed quickly, then let go. "You can call me Gary," he said.

"And I'm Mary," she said. "Do you live in the neighborhood?"

He nodded, but had a hard time meeting her eyes. "Yes, our properties actually touch lines on the east side of the back of your lot," he said. "Jeannine used to call us kitty-corner neighbors."

"Well, neighbor, come in and make yourself comfortable," she said, guiding them into the chairs in the living room.

She offered Gary a chair that was facing one of the concealed cameras and she sat across from him on the love seat.

"Well, it's nice to meet a new neighbor," Ian added, following them and sitting on the arm of the love seat. "As you know, we're brand new here."

73

"Yes. I mean, I know. I mean, that's why I came by, actually," he stammered. "I knew the Aldens owned this place, Bradley and Jeannine. I saw the lights, from my kitchen. I wondered, you know, who you were. Why you were here. Because I didn't think Bradley wanted to ever sell his house."

Mary shook her head. "Oh, no, they still own it," she said. "Bradley is letting us rent it from him for a while. We're newlyweds and still haven't quite got ourselves situated."

"Oh," he said, looking around nervously. "I'm sorry, I shouldn't be here. I mean, newlyweds, company is the last thing you'd want."

Ian moved onto the love seat, put his arm around Mary's shoulders and drew her close. "I have to tell you, with a wife like Mary, I plan on being a newlywed 'til my dying day."

Mary leaned her head on Ian's shoulder. "Now that was sweet," she said. "So, Gary, are you married?"

He lifted his head to look at Mary, then shook it quickly and addressed Ian. "No, I'm divorced," he said. "I wasn't real good with words, like you are. I think she got bored with me."

"Oh, I'm so sorry," Mary said.

Gary shrugged. "I'm okay now," he said, shrugging. "I have lots of friends and my practice, so I keep real busy."

Ian nodded. "Good for you," he said. "So, are you a good dentist? I'm sure we'll be looking for one soon enough."

Laughing, Gary nodded. "I've never had a patient complain yet," he said.

"Well, that's a fine recommendation then, isn't it?" Ian replied, giving Mary a quick squeeze. "And what do you suggest the proper dental hygiene is for a woman who's expecting?"

Gary looked straight at Mary. "You're pregnant?" he asked, and then blushed again. "I mean, congratulations."

Mary smiled. "Well, actually, we were trying to keep it a secret for a little bit longer," she said, looking up at Ian. "But someone wants to shout it from the rooftops."

He grinned at her. "It just keeps slipping out," he laughed.

Gary stood. "Well, that's just, that's great," he said. "You should be really happy. I, I'd better go now."

Mary and Ian both stood. "We'll walk you out," he said.

Bradley sat back in his office chair. He could watch the meeting through the wireless camera system and hear the discussion in the next room through both the laptop and the camera microphones. He hadn't seen Gary in years. The conversation Ian and Mary shared with Gary reminded him of so many evenings Gary and his wife, Beverly, had come over and chatted with Jeannine and him. And then, after his divorce, Gary had sought their company most nights and they all became good friends.

Jeannine had felt sorry for Gary because he was so shy and awkward around women and his divorce certainly hadn't helped increase his self-esteem. Even though Gary was older than they were, he and Jeannine seemed to fill the roles of older siblings, offering advice and listening to his problems.

But when he had problems, Gary was the first one to step up. He had even been kind enough to help Bradley financially when he had continued his search for Jeannine. He knew the house wouldn't still have been his without Gary's help.

Bradley ran his hand through his hair and closed his eyes for a moment. But he knew those old memories weren't the cause for the unsettled feelings near his heart. When Ian had announced Mary was pregnant, he immediately remembered his dream. In it Mary had been eight months pregnant. He could easily recall the pressure of her swollen body against his, the feeling of their child moving against him when they were embracing and the rightness of her in his arms. But at the end of the dream she had walked away, married to someone else.

All because he had chosen Jeannine. He suddenly sat up straight.

Had that been a warning?

He had never considered himself superstitious, but in his dream Mary told him she was married to Mike, a ghost. Would you have to be dead in order to be married to a ghost? Was Mary's life at risk because of Jeannine's investigation?

He leaned forward in his chair and placed his head in his hands. What were his choices at this point? Jeannine was Mary's client and there was no way Mary would drop the case. He knew her well enough to know she would not be worried about her own safety.

Sitting back up in the chair, he scanned the monitor and found her in the camera screen in the front hall. She was smiling at Gary and waving goodbye.

"What do you want from me, Mary O'Reilly?" he whispered, at the screen.

He could hear her response in his mind. *"Trust me."*

He would just have to have faith. Trust Mary. That's what she had asked for, and if it killed him, he would trust her.

Once Gary left, Mary hurried over to the computer. She moved the screen back to face the room and unclicked the mute button.

"So, did you hear the conversation?" she asked.

Bradley nodded. "Yeah, but you don't have to worry about Gary," he said. "He's as good as gold. He actually helped me when I was searching for Jeannine."

"So, you wouldn't put him on your list?" Ian asked.

"No, never," Bradley said. "I'd trust him with my life."

Chapter Eleven

Mary came out of the bathroom dressed in her favorite sleeping attire, a large t-shirt and sweatpants, turned off the lights and climbed onto the bed. She felt a little strange sleeping in the master bedroom, the same bed Bradley and Jeannine had shared. But Ian had suggested that it would probably be the best place for her because Jeannine would gravitate to that room. She moved the pillows against the headboard, leaned back against them and pulled her laptop into her lap.

She powered it on and clicked on the video conferencing software. In a moment she was connected with Bradley who was still sitting at his desk.

"Planning on staying up all night, Chief?" she teased.

"I was hoping you'd call," he replied. "How are you doing?"

The sound of his voice, deep and slightly rough, was heightened by the intimacy of sitting in his bed in the darkened bedroom. Mary felt it wash over her like a silken wave.

"I'm good," she said, keeping her voice to a whisper. "I like your house."

"I dreamt about you in my house," he said.

Laughing softly, she snuggled against the pillows. "Was I chasing bad guys?"

He chuckled. "No, actually, you were cooking dinner."

"Well, how domestic of me."

"Extremely," he said. "And, I have to tell you, exceptionally sexy."

She felt her cheeks burn and was grateful of the darkened room. "How is cooking dinner sexy?"

"Well, it was a pot roast," he replied with a quiet laughter.

"Oh, well then, I totally understand," she said. "Pot roast can be a stimulating experience."

"Exactly! I came into the house and you were standing in front of the stove. In my dream, I initially thought you were Jeannine, but then when I slid my arms around you and pulled you into my arms, I discovered it was you," he said.

"Were you disappointed?"

"No, I was confused at first, but once you slipped your arms around my neck and kissed me, I knew everything was perfect."

"I kissed you? Sounds like I was being a little assertive."

"Have I mentioned how much I like assertive women?"

She chuckled.

"And when you were locked in my arms, I felt our baby move against me and I knew nothing could compare with that moment."

"I was pregnant? You could have mentioned that. Was I really fat?"

"You were perfect," he whispered slowly, his voice husky and his eyes meeting hers. "Absolutely perfect."

She took a deep breath and slowly released it, feeling her body respond to his words. "Bradley, I…"

"Wait, Mary," he said. "Let me tell you the rest of the dream."

"Okay."

"You pulled away from me to stir something on the stove."

"I'm an idiot," Mary muttered.

"Pardon me?"

"Oh, nothing, please continue."

"That's when I noticed that Jeannine was sitting at the kitchen table," he said. "She told me she'd been dead for eight years."

"What did I do?"

"You invited her to dinner," he replied, a small smile on his lips.

"Well, of course I did," she said. "That was the only polite thing to do."

"Yes, I'm sure Miss Manners has something about dead wives and inviting them to dinner," he said.

Her laughter bubbled out. "Of course she does."

Bradley paused for a moment, just to study her. Her eyes were sparkling and her mouth was turned up in an adorable smile. Her lips were so kissable, especially when she was laughing. He had given her far too few reasons to laugh lately. Taking a deep breath, he continued. "That's when Jeannine reminded me of our conversation on New Year's Eve," he said.

Mary inhaled softly.

"She reminded me that you told me the truth," he said. "But I wasn't listening. She reminded me that not only did you save my life; you had always been honest and open with me. She reminded me what an idiot I'd been."

"I couldn't tell you anything else," she said. "I wanted to, really, but I couldn't."

"Yeah, I see that now," he said. "I just wanted to let you know why I came knocking on your door at two o'clock in the morning. I had to apologize. I had to see in your eyes that you forgave me, that you still loved me. That is wasn't too late."

"And then Ian answered the door," she said, nodding in understanding.

"And once again, I opted to act like an idiot rather than trust you," he said. "If it helps, I was totally miserable on my drive home and nearly destroyed my living room when I got there by throwing my slippers across the room."

"Slippers?"

"Yeah, I was in a hurry, so I just slipped on jeans and slippers."

"But there was an ice storm…"

"I figured that out when I stepped out of my car into a snow drift and then nearly killed myself slipping across your porch," he confessed. "When Ian opened the door, I was laying on my stomach, inching my way to your door."

Mary put a hand over her mouth to hold back the laughter.

"Are you laughing at me?" he asked.

She shook her head, too afraid to move her hand for fear the laughter would escape.

"Are you lying to me?" he asked, his mouth turned up in a smile and his eyes sharing the joke with her.

She nodded her head, still covering her mouth.

His face sobered and he looked at her with such intensity that her laughter was dispelled. Her heart accelerated and she felt a warm rush throughout her body.

"Do you still love me?" he asked.

A single tear slipped down her cheek and she nodded slowly. "I never stopped," she whispered.

He took a deep breath. "It's probably a good thing I'm not there right now," he said. "It would be hard to walk away from you tonight, Mary."

Nodding, she met his eyes. "It would be hard to ask you to," she whispered.

His jaw tightened for a moment and then he relaxed. "Go to bed, Mary," he said softly. "And have sweet dreams."

"I will," she said. "Good night, Bradley."

She disconnected the call, lay back against the pillows and sighed. "I love you Bradley Alden," she said aloud.

Smiling, Bradley adjusted the speaker on the bedroom's camera, she deserved a little privacy. "I love you too, Mary O'Reilly," he whispered.

Chapter Twelve

The house was dark, but she was used to walking through it with only the streetlights illuminating the rooms. She remembered all of those times when she woke in the middle of the night and couldn't sleep. She'd come downstairs, sit in the recliner and talk to her unborn child. Sharing her hopes and her fears. Whispering to the baby about Bradley and the silly things he was already worrying about. Letting the baby know how special she was and how much she was wanted.

Jeannine looked around the kitchen. She remembered finding the kitchen clock at a flea market. She could picture herself halfway up a ladder, painting the walls and working until midnight sewing the curtains. The refrigerator door was clean now, but it used to be filled with letters, take-out menus and photos. She strolled next to the counters, remembering the dishes lovingly created and the holiday feasts that were sometimes disasters, and smiled.

Am I haunting my home? she wondered. *Is this what a ghost does?*

Strolling into the living room she saw Ian sprawled on the couch, a myriad of computer screens and blinking consoles in front of him. His attention was drawn to one specific screen and as she approached to get a better look, he sat up and looked at her over the back of the couch.

"Good, it's you," he said.

Jeannine jumped back. "You startled me," she confessed.

"Oh, sorry," he replied with a grin. "I've been following your magnetic impulses since you entered the kitchen. I was hoping it was you, not that it wouldn't be brilliant if there was another ghost living here."

"I don't know if I want a ghost living in my house," Jeannine protested.

Ian looked at her and raised one eyebrow.

"Oh, yeah, I guess I am that ghost," she said with a sigh. "Really, it's hard to get used to."

"So, have you ever had any psychic phenomena in this house?" he asked.

She put her hands on her hips and shook her head. "Do you really think Bradley would allow for something like that in his house?" she teased.

"Ach, no, I forgot whose house I was speaking about," he replied. "No ghost would be so daring."

She glided closer to him, and glanced over her shoulder. "Although, I have to admit there were a couple of times when I thought I saw someone out of the corner of my eye, but when I turned no one was there."

"What time of the day?"

"Usually during the night, when I couldn't sleep," she said.

"Upstairs or downstairs," he asked, grabbing a pad and pencil.

"Upstairs," she replied. "But it was probably nothing. Beverly Copper and her first husband had this house built for them, then they got divorced and she married Gary."

"Well, perhaps it was built on an old graveyard," Ian suggested, referring to the scenario from an old horror show.

Jeannine laughed. "Well, then I'd be sure not to turn the television on late at night."

Ian thought about the irony of his situation. Here he was, lying on a coach, speaking with the ghost of a lovely woman who was hovering several inches in the air and discussing a classic horror flick with him. *Life was pretty damn brilliant!*

"What are you thinking?" Jeannine asked.

"I was just thinking about the whole situation here," he said. "It's a little bit unusual."

She laughed. "To say the least."

"Can I ask you a question?"

She nodded her assent.

"How is it?" he asked. "Being a ghost. What does it feel like?"

Glancing away from him, she caught sight of the window. Snow was falling and it could only be seen in the beams from the streetlights. *Is that what eternity was like?* she wondered. *You're only aware of the small part you're living, but there is so much more beyond what you can see.*

"When you were a child were you ever sick with something that was contagious, like chicken pox or measles?" she finally asked, turning to look at him. "You really weren't sick anymore, but because you were still contagious, you had to stay inside."

She walked over to the window and stared outside. "You sat next to the window, watching all of your friends playing together, and you wanted to be with them," she said. "You could see them, hear them and even, if you were lucky, laugh with them. But you couldn't be with them. You were always separated from them."

Pausing, she turned to look at him. "A thin piece of glass or the thin veil between life and death, the separation is the same."

Ian stood up and walked over next to her. "It sounds lonely," he said.

"It is. I'm not really here with the people I love, I'm just a shadow. I haven't moved on to be with the family and friends who have gone before me. I'm stuck in the middle."

"Waiting for your business to be resolved," he said. "It must be frustrating to have to wait."

"And some have to wait longer than others," she said sadly. "If you don't mind, I think I'm just going to walk around a bit."

He nodded. "I'll see you tomorrow," he said.

"Pleasant dreams, Ian," she said and faded away into the night.

Although the room was still dark, the lights from the console helped to guide him back to the couch. Lying down, he propped his head on his arm and stared out the window into the sparkling snowflakes dancing in the light. A poem he had learned in his youth came to mind. The author was Emily Bronte, but he thought Jeannine could have written the lines.

The night is darkening round me,
The wild winds coldly blow;
But a tyrant spell has bound me
And I cannot, cannot go.

"We'll help you break the spell, Jeannine," he whispered. "I promise."

Jeannine glided slowly up the stairs to the second floor. She entered the bedroom she used to use as a sewing room and looked around. Things were as they had been eight years ago. Her favorite books still lined the shelves and some unfinished craft projects sat in a plastic tub in the corner of the room. Then she turned and saw the half-finished quilt lying on the cutting table. She glided over to it and was overcome with a fresh wave of grief. She had actually talked Bradley into entering a fabric store with her because she wanted him to help her pick out the perfect fabric for their baby girl.

Bradley went immediately to the fleece section, pulling out bolts of fabrics that represented his favorite sports teams.

"We are not going to wrap our delicate baby girl in a blanket that says 'Da Bears,'" Jeannine had insisted.

He pulled out another bolt. "How about the Cubs?" he asked hopefully.

She had put her hands on her hips and just stared at him. Sighing, he put the bolts back in place. "Okay, where do you want me to look?" he asked.

She took his hand and let him over to the soft cotton flannels. Before he could say a word, she lifted a piece of the material and stroked it against his cheek.

"The fleece was soft too," he grumbled, but he took the soft pink fabric and rubbed it between his thumb and forefinger. "But this will definitely match the nursery better."

It took them nearly forty-five minutes to come up with the perfect combination of materials for the quilt, but Bradley was grinning at her as he carried an armload of fabric laden bolts to the cutting table. "It's going to look great," he said. "She's going to love it."

Jeannine shook her head sadly and moved away from the cutting table. She would never get to hold her baby girl in that quilt. A soft cry escaped her lips and for the first time in a long time, she allowed herself to weep for her loss.

She slowly glided out of the sewing room and down the dark hallway. She moved toward the master bedroom, but could hear Mary's voice, so she continued on. The nursery was at the end of the hall. Could she bear to enter it and see the cans of paint sitting unused, the crib still boxed and leaning against the wall, the boxes of baby paraphernalia she had already purchased once they knew they were having a girl?

Yes! She had to see it. She had to look it over and make herself remember what happened. She had to know.

She slipped into the room, looked around and burst into tears.

Mary laid her laptop on the nightstand next to the bed and snuggled into the pillows. "I love you Bradley Alden," she said and sighed with contentment.

Then she heard it. She sat up in the bed and listened for a moment, to be sure it just wasn't the sound of the wind against the house. No, it was definitely the sound of someone crying.

She slipped from the bed and hurried out of the room. The hallway was dark, but there was enough light to find her way. The noise was coming from the room at the end of the hall. She hadn't been in that room yet. Ian had placed the camera in that one, while she took the sewing room.

She placed her hand on the knob and slowly opened the door. Light from the lampposts softly illuminated the room. Mary turned and saw Jeannine seated on a rocking chair in the corner of the room. She had her head bowed into her hands and her cries were heartbreaking.

"Jeannine, what's wrong?" Mary asked, moving forward and kneeling next to the chair.

Jeannine looked up and for a moment didn't speak. Her translucent face was covered in tears; her body was shaking with emotion. Finally she took a deep shuddering breath. "The room is pink," she whispered. "He still painted it pink."

Mary looked around the room; it was painted a soft pink with white trim. A crib was set up in the corner of the room with a pink baby mobile hanging above it. A matching changing table was against another wall, a stuffed lamb propped in the corner. Shelves filled with other stuffed animals were attached to the wall across from the crib.

"Bradley did this?" Mary asked, her voice filled with emotion.

"The room was a mess," Jeannine said. "Nothing was put together. Nothing was arranged. Why did he do this?"

"So it would be ready when you and the baby came home," Mary replied, her eyes filling with tears. "He loved you so much."

Jeannine nodded and met Mary's eyes. "He's a good man," she said. "He might occasionally do something stupid, but he's a good man."

Mary smiled and shook her head in agreement. "Yes, he is."

"I like you, Mary," she continued. "I think you and I would have been friends if we met before I died."

"I'd like to think we are friends anyway," Mary said.

Jeannine smiled now. "Yes. Yes, we are," she agreed. "So, friend, I want you to promise me two things. I want you to love him with all your heart."

Mary nodded her head in agreement. "I can do that."

"And I want you to take that baby quilt in the sewing room and finish it for me," she said. "I don't know why, but it's important to me."

"I promise," Mary agreed. "I'll even have my mom help me."

Jeannine angled her head in confusion.

"Well, if I do it by myself, I have no idea what it will look like when it's done," she said with a smile. "I usually injure myself when I'm anywhere near a thread and needle. It's even more dangerous than police work."

Jeannine laughed. "Bradley's a lucky man to have found such a wonderful woman to love."

"Bradley is exceptionally lucky, because he found two wonderful women to love him," Mary added.

Jeannine smiled. "Thank you, Mary," she whispered and then she faded away.

Chapter Thirteen

The next day dawned bright and sunny. Mary was downstairs in the kitchen sipping a can of Diet Pepsi and putting on the kettle for Ian by seven o'clock. Remembering Ian's appetite, she opened the cabinet and pulled out the package of oatmeal and a large measuring cup. When she closed the door, Jeannine was standing on the other side of it.

Mary jumped. "Do you ghosts do that on purpose?" she asked.

Jeannine grinned. "Do what Mary?"

"I thought so," Mary replied. "So, what shall we do today?"

Just then she heard a rattle on the kitchen door and voices on the other side.

"It's too goldarned early for folks to be up," Stanley growled. "I told you we didn't have to leave at the butt-crack of dawn."

"Listen to me, Stanley Wagner, if you can't get your body out of bed by five o'clock, then I'll drive myself in the future," Rosie said. "But then you won't be able to eat half of the muffins on the way here."

"Well, I was hungry," he muttered. "Getting up early does that to a man."

Jeannine turned to Mary. "Are they always like this?" she asked.

Laughing, Mary nodded as she walked across the room. "Sometimes they're even worse."

She opened the door and invited them in. "Well, thank goodness you finally made it," she said with a grin. "I've been waiting for hours and I hope you didn't eat all of the muffins."

"That's enough of that, Miss Sassy Pants," Stanley said.

Rosie smiled at Mary and placed the basket of muffins on the counter. She opened up the towel covering the basket, picked up a muffin and handed it to Mary.

"No, Mary, don't eat it," Jeannine screamed, gliding across the room toward her.

Mary jumped back and dropped the muffin on to the counter.

"What's wrong, Mary?" Rosie asked. "Was the muffin too hot?"

"You goose, we just drove an hour to get here," Stanley said. "The muffin couldn't be hot. There's something else going on."

Mary turned to Jeannine, who was standing next to the counter staring at the muffin.

"What happened, Jeannine?"

"Who is she talking to, Stanley?" Rosie asked.

"Shhhh, listen for a minute," he replied.

Jeannine looked up at Mary. "There was something about the muffin, a muffin," she said. "I remember a muffin just before I was taken from the house."

94

"What else do you remember?"

Jeannine closed her eyes for a moment, concentrating on why the muffin seemed so dangerous. Finally, she opened them and shrugged. "Nothing, I can't remember anything else."

"Mary, dear, you're talking to the air," Rosie said. "Do you want me to get you a glass of water?"

Mary turned back to Rosie and Stanley who stood frozen in the same positions they had been in when she dropped the muffin. "I'm sorry," she said. "Bradley's wife, Jeannine, is here in the room with us."

Rosie gasped and turned to Stanley. "She's imagining things," she whispered.

"No she's not, she's talking about a ghost," he replied.

Rosie turned back to Mary. "Really? Is there a ghost in the room with us? I've never been in a room with a ghost," she said, then paused for a moment. "Or perhaps I should say I've never been aware that I was in a room with a ghost, because they are invisible after all. Oh, dear, I've been talking about her as if she weren't here. How rude of me."

She walked over, stood next to Mary and then turned in the general direction of where Mary had been addressing Jeannine. "Hello," she said loudly and slowly. "My name is Rosie and I'm a friend of Mary's."

"She dead, not deaf," Stanley growled.

"I'm sure there have been deaf ghosts before," Rosie countered. "Besides, I wanted to be sure she knew I was a friend."

"Well, the fact that Mary let us in her home at seven a.m. in the morning must tell her that we ain't strangers."

Jeannine chuckled. "Your friends are quite a combination."

Mary nodded. "Yes, they are."

"Did she hear me?" Rosie asked Mary.

"Yes, she did, and she thinks you are delightful."

Rosie beamed and turned to Stanley. "She thinks I'm delightful."

"Well, you are delightful," he agreed crossly. "But you're also dingy."

Rosie's cheeks turned pink. "Why thank you, Stanley."

"Thank you, Stanley, for what?" Ian asked, walking into the room still dressed in his pajamas.

He spied the basket of muffins, pulled one out and took a big bite. "Oh, these are heavenly," he moaned. "Rosie, did you make these?"

Rosie nodded. "Just baked them fresh this morning."

Ian went down on one knee in front of her. "Rosie, my darling, will you marry me?" he asked.

"Dang Scottish Casanova," Stanley said, moving over next to Rosie. "Ain't you got enough on your hands being married to Mary and having a fiancée back home?"

"I'd leave them all for baking like this," he teased. "So, Rosie do you want to run away with me to Las Vegas? We could get married tomorrow."

Rosie tittered. "Well, Ian..."

"She ain't getting married to no one," Stanley said. "Least of all, not some foreigner."

"Ah, I see I have a contender for the lady's charms," Ian said, raising one eyebrow in Stanley's direction.

"I ain't saying you do and I ain't saying you don't," he replied. "I'm just saying right now we got a murder to solve and standing around yacking ain't solving nothing."

Ian stood up, grabbed another muffin and leaned against the counter. "Aye, you have the right of it, Stanley," he said. "What are we up to today?"

"Muffins," Mary said, picking up a muffin from the basket on the counter. "Jeannine took one look at the muffin Rosie gave me and screamed at me to drop it."

Ian paused halfway through another bite of muffin and turned to Jeannine. "There's something wrong with the muffins?"

Jeannine chuckled. "No, something happened. A memory, a flashback, I don't know. But when I saw Mary pick up the muffin I freaked out."

"He can see Jeannine too?" Rosie asked.

"Aye, I can see Jeannine and you're missing out if you can't, for she's lovely as a summer morning," he said.

"For a dead person," Jeannine quipped.

Ian laughed. "Aye, you have me there. So, now, what do we do with this memory? Do you have any idea why muffins terrify you?"

She shook her head. "No, I keep hitting a wall every time I try to remember."

He nodded. "Well, then, there's only one thing we can do."

"And what's that?" Mary asked.

He took another large bite of muffin. "Hypnotize her," he said. "And see if we can break down the wall."

"You can hypnotize a ghost?" Rosie asked.

Ian shrugged. "Don't know if it's ever been done before," he said. "But we can try. How does that sound to you?"

Jeannine stared at Ian for a moment. "You're not going to make me do the chicken dance, are you?"

Muffin crumbs flew across the kitchen counter as Ian choked on his laughter. Mary came up behind him and patted him on the back, trying to hold back her own laughter.

"No," he choked. "Nothing like that. Serious, professional hypnotism."

Jeannine smiled at him. "Well, then professor, I'll place myself in your capable hands."

Chapter Fourteen

Mike was bored. He didn't understand why he wasn't able to follow Mary to Sycamore. Whenever he tried to picture her in his mind, he ended up in her empty house. So he walked through the rooms and watched out the windows. He played the radio and even found himself reading through Ian's notes on paranormal entities.

Often the ghost doesn't realize he's haunting an establishment. Sometimes a ghost has a connection to a place and the connection has him returning time and time again. Once there, the ghost finds itself bored and wanders aimlessly throughout the house.

"Damn, I'm haunting Mary's house," he said when the realization hit him. "If I don't get something to do I'm going to drive myself crazy."

Moments later, he heard the front door open. "Excellent, a burglar," he said, moving toward the front of the house. "I'll take care of him."

To his dismay, it wasn't a criminal. In fact, it was quite the opposite. Police Chief Bradley Alden flipped on the light after letting himself into Mary's house. He walked to the kitchen and filled a pitcher with water.

"Really? You're just watering her plants?" Mike said. "Is that the best use of taxpayers' money?"

Because Bradley couldn't hear Mike, he just went about his business, watering the plants.

"Well, this is absolutely no fun," Mike said, and then a grin appeared on his face. "But I could make it more interesting."

Mike moved closer to Bradley, and as Bradley tipped the pitcher to pour water into the pot, Mike pushed the pot a few inches. Water splashed on the table top. "Damn, how did I do that?" Bradley asked.

He put the pitcher down and went to the kitchen for a dish towel to wipe up the mess. Then he picked the pitcher up again and Mike moved the pot again. Bradley stopped mid-pour, saving the table from another soaking. He looked slowly around the room and then spoke. "I'll tell Mary the water stain on her favorite antique table was your fault."

Mike moved the pot back in place.

"Thank you," Bradley said, finally watering the plant. "So, I'm guessing you must be Mike. I don't think we've ever been formally introduced. I'm Bradley."

The white board on the refrigerator floated across the room. "NICE TO MEET YOU" appeared slowly as an unseen hand moved the black marker back and forth.

"It would be a hell of a lot easier if I could see and hear you," Bradley said.

"FOR ME TOO," the marker printed. Then Mike remembered something else Ian had written. He glided across the room, picked up the notebook and flipped it to the proper page.

"You want me to read something?" Bradley asked. "You want me to read the notebook?"

"This isn't an adventure of Lassie," Mike grumbled. "Of course, I want you to read the notebook. Why else would I be flipping it open in front of you?"

Unaware of Mike's comments, Bradley picked the notebook up and read the page.

Some researchers believe that subjects must be born with a substantial amount of ESP or have had some kind of near-death experience in order to acquire the ability to see and communicate with spirits of the deceased or ghosts. However, during a recent study of pre-school children who were placed in an atmosphere highly conducive to paranormal activity, ninety percent of those children were able to communicate with ghosts. This leads me to the conclusion that the ability to see ghosts lies within our own psyche. As children no one has prejudiced us against the idea of being able to see ghosts and therefore, we open our minds and are willing to see them. As we age, more encumbrances are placed upon our conscious as well as our subconscious, and we close our minds to the possibility of seeing ghosts. My final conclusion is one will be able to see ghosts if one only allows one's conscious and subconscious to accept their existence as part of reality and are willing to see them.

He sat down on Mary's couch and pondered Ian's words. "Well, it certainly makes sense," Bradley said. "I can see ghosts."

"Yeah, but only if we want you to see us," Mike said. "There's not a lot of Mary O'Reillys in the world."

Bradley thought back to his first encounters with ghosts. Earl was his first experience, a ghost from the Civil War who would visit Mary every night at midnight, seeking her help. Bradley had spent the night at Mary's because she had been hurt and he didn't want her to be alone. He woke when the clock struck midnight and he heard someone walking up her basement stairs. Gun drawn, he angled himself so he would see the intruder as soon as the door opened. The door had been bolted shut, but the intruder forced it open, ripping the bolt from its casing in the door. The door swung open and Bradley yelled out, identifying himself as a law enforcement officer. But there was no one there.

He watched, open mouthed, as he heard the thumping footsteps make their way up the stairs to the second floor, but there was no one there to make the sounds. Mary woke up long enough to tell him it was just Earl, and to assure him that when Earl discovered Mary wasn't upstairs, he'd just turn around and leave.

Sure enough, a few moments later, Bradley heard the returning footfalls and once again, saw no one.

He shook his head and refused to believe what he had just seen. "But there are no such things as ghosts," he had insisted.

Mary just shrugged and said, "Oh, yeah, I keep forgetting."

He chuckled at the memory. Boy, did he have a lot to learn.

Then, just a few days later, he learned that when he was in contact with Mary he was able to not only hear, but see ghosts. The first ghost had been the president of the local bank who had been murdered, but it had been made to look like a suicide. He had been crying in Mary's basement and, because he had insisted, she called him before she went down and investigated. She told him someone was crying, but he couldn't hear anything. She had patted his arm in sympathy and he realized he could hear the crying when she touched him.

If he could hear by a simple touch, surely he could see ghosts if he just concentrated.

He closed his eyes and told himself that he could see ghosts. Then he opened them...the room was still empty.

"Mike, are you still here?" he called out.

"YES – I AM," he wrote on the white board.

"Okay, it's not working yet," Bradley said. "But I'm trying."

He closed his eyes again and this time he squeezed them tight. "I believe, I believe, I believe."

He opened his eyes and looked past Mike into the room. "Mike?"

"Well, that worked," Mike said, rolling his eyes. "It's obvious you have some kind of mental block. Maybe we need to use psychology to help you with this problem."

"WAIT HERE – I HAVE AN IDEA," he wrote on the board.

A moment later Mike materialized in Mary's room. "She's got to have something around here that will work," he said as he scanned her room.

Then he saw the vase filled with small colored glass stones. He lifted one of the stones out; it was dark blue and had a darker swirl in the middle of it. "Perfect," he said. "Looks pretty mystic to me."

He started to walk out of the room when he noticed the bathroom door was ajar. The only rule the ghosts who visited Mary had was to not appear to her in the bathroom. *But Mary isn't here,* he reasoned.

He quickly glided across the room and stopped at the bathroom doorway. Peering inside, he could see her vanity filled with soaps, creams and other beauty products. Then he saw her shower. It was a beautiful block of glass walls and chrome. It had multiple shower heads and jets placed on the walls.

"No wonder she doesn't want anyone in here," he said. "She doesn't want to share."

He glided into the bathroom and picked up a bar of soap. Entering the shower, he sung a little tune to himself as he turned to the glass wall facing toward the bathroom and drew the soap across the glass a number of times. Then he pulled a towel from a nearby shelf and hung it strategically over the chrome bar in the shower.

"There we are," he said with a grin. "A nice welcome home for Mary."

A few moments later he was down in the living room, standing in front of Bradley with the white board. "I'M BACK," he wrote.

"What took you so long?" Bradley asked.

"HAD TO USE THE BATHROOM," he responded in print. "I HAVE SOMETHING FOR YOU. IT SHOULD HELP."

A dark blue stone floated across the room and landed in Bradley's hand. "What's this?"

"Oh, just a piece of glass I found in Mary's room," Mike said aloud. "But it's enough to fool you into believing in the powers you already possess."

"A GIFT TO MARY FROM IAN. ANCIENT DIVINATION STONE. HELPS YOU CONTACT SPIRITS," he wrote.

"Really," Bradley said, hefting it in his hand. "What am I supposed to do with it?"

"Whip it across the room and see if anyone screams," Mike said.

"JUST RUB IT AND YOU CAN SEE GHOSTS. WORKED FOR HUNDREDS OF YEARS," he wrote.

"Just rub it," he read aloud. He rubbed the stone, concentrating on whatever power it had to open up the unknown. "This little stone is going to change my life. Just like Mary did."

"Yeah, meeting Mary does that to a guy."

Shocked, Bradley looked up to see a fairly young man standing in front of him. But he was translucent.

"Damn, it worked," Bradley said in awe. "Are you Mike?"

Mike nodded. "Yeah, Chief, nice to meet you."

Bradley took a good look at Mike. He was a young man in prime condition and looked like he could have posed for one of those fireman calendars. "I had hoped you were old and fat," Bradley said.

Mike snorted. "Yeah, and I wish I was still alive, so we both lose."

Bradley sobered. "Hey, I'm sorry…"

"No, don't worry about it," Mike said. "I'm getting used to it. Besides, I get to pop in on Mary any time I feel like it. Day or night."

"Are you trying to start something here?" Bradley asked.

"Sure, I'll do anything for a little excitement."

Bradley paused for a moment. Having Mike around might be a solution to another problem facing his department. "Can you see other ghosts?" he asked.

"Sometimes," Mike replied. "Just depends."

"Depends on what?"

"Depends if I can see them or not," Mike said, rolling his eyes. "Listen, I'm fairly new to this whole ghost thing, so I'm not up on all the rules. Sometimes I see them and sometimes I don't."

Bradley stood up and faced Mike. "Actually, I could use your help. We think we have an arsonist in town," Bradley said. "There's been a flurry of burning barns across the county. We have no motive, they all seem like random acts, but yesterday we found a body in the ruins of one of the barns. Want to take a look?"

"You asking me to investigate an arson scene, talk to a potential victim and help you solve a murder?" he asked.

Bradley nodded. "Yes, I am. You interested?"

"Hell, yes, I'm interested," he said. "You can water those plants later. Come on; let's catch us some bad guys."

"Yeah, and on the way, we can talk about this dropping in on Mary thing," Bradley said, as he walked out the door.

Chapter Fifteen

"Okay Jeannine," Ian said. "Let's try this one more time."

Jeannine nodded. "I'm so sorry, Ian. I just can't seem to get this right."

"That's okay," he said. "I suppose this is harder when you don't have a body."

Jeannine hovered above the couch in a horizontal position and took a deep breath. "I'm ready."

The curtains had been drawn and the lights had been turned low. Stanley and Rosie sat across the room, keeping an eye on the doors in case they had any surprise visitors. Mary sat in a chair alongside the back of the couch, ready to take notes.

Ian pulled his chair closer to the couch and leaned forward. "Now Jeannine, I want you to clear your mind," he said calmly. "Picture yourself on a white fluffy cloud floating above the earth with blue sky all around you. It's warm on your skin and you feel totally at ease."

Jeannine nodded and closed her eyes. She thought about the things Ian had suggested to her. Beautiful blue skies and fluffy white clouds. She inhaled deeply. She was slowly drifting. Her mind was clear. She was ready for Ian's hypnotic suggestion.

She breathed in slowly, and picked up a fresh, almost salty fragrance. *Was that a scented candle?* she wondered. She could hear noises in the distance, it sounded like a crowd of people. *Has Stanley turned the television on?* Then she heard the distinct roar of an airplane.

Airplane?

Jeannine opened her eyes and looked around. *Crap!* She was above Hawaii, floating in one of the clouds near the island of Oahu. She and Bradley had gone there when they were newlyweds. But that was not where she was supposed to be now.

She closed her eyes and focused back on her house. Back on the living room couch. Back with Ian, Mary, Rosie and Stanley.

"Aye, well, she's back now," she heard Ian say.

She opened her eyes and looked around. Yes, she was back in her living room.

"So, where did you go this time?" Mary asked, leaning over the back of the couch.

"Hawaii," she replied. "It's really lovely this time of year."

"Well, that's better than Alaska," Mary said.

"I'm grateful for the suggestion of blue skies and warmth. The whole 'everything around you is white' was not as enjoyable."

She turned to Ian. "I'm so sorry," she said. "I do everything you ask me to do and poof, I end up somewhere else."

"It's not your fault," he said. "You have no body to anchor you down."

"But there has to be a way," she said. "I need to remember."

"I have a suggestion," Mary said.

"I'm open to just about anything," he replied.

"Let me be the body for Jeannine. Hypnotize both of us."

Rosie shook her head. "Oh, no," she said. "I've seen movies like that, where spirits inhabit someone else's body. Bad things always happen to them, Mary."

Mary smiled at Rosie. "But, Rosie, Jeannine and I are friends," she said. "It won't be like that."

"Can't say I'm crazy about the idea either," Stanley said. "What's to say once she's in there, she'll be able to get out?"

"I've seen it happen a time or two at a séance," Ian said. "The medium opens herself up and the spirit is able to enter her body. It's called channeling. But it can be dangerous because you don't know what kind of spirit might enter your body."

Jeannine looked confused. "What do you mean, kind of spirit?" she asked. "The dead kind, right?"

"Well, actually, there are good spirits and there are evil spirits," Ian explained. "Some evil spirits are tortured souls who led the kind of life that have them trapped here on earth. Some, from what I understand, never got the chance to have bodies and just hover around, waiting for a chance to try one on for size."

"I never heard that," Stanley said. "Where would they hang out?"

"Places where people are apt to give up control of their bodies," he said. "Like the neighborhood pub where I've seen many a lad drink so much alcohol, he has no idea where he is or what he's about. He's a perfect victim for that kind of visitor."

Rosie cocked her head to the side, considering what Ian had just said. "So, those people who do crazy things when they're drunk and can't remember anything about it. It might be because someone else is in there with them?"

Ian shrugged. "I can't tell you for sure," he said. "But, that's the theory I've heard."

"Well, I'm not going to get drunk," Mary said. "I'm just going to sit back and share my body with Jeannine's spirit for a little bit. And with all of you here, I'm sure I'll be safe."

"What do you think, Jeannine?" Ian asked.

"I'd be very grateful to Mary if it works," she said. "I really think it's the only way we are going to solve my murder."

Ian stood up and checked his computer. "Okay, I think it best we not advertise what we're doing over the cameras," he said.

"No, I don't think either Sean or Bradley would be happy with this experiment," Mary agreed, then she clapped her hand over her mouth. "Have they been listening in?"

Ian clicked on a few screens and then shook his head. "No, luck is with us. They've both been offline for at least an hour," he said. "Stanley, can you do me a favor and cover that camera with a paper sack? I'll turn down the sound and send a message out that we've encountered a slight problem with the living room camera, but we'll have it fixed in a trice."

A few minutes later, the camera was covered and Ian had set up another one to record the session.

"Why didn't you have that set up when Jeannine was being hypnotized?" Rosie asked.

"Because I couldn't capture Jeannine's voice or form on the camera," Ian explained. "And now I'll be able to do both."

"And I don't think I'll be available to take notes," Mary added, and then turned to Ian. "What will I be feeling?"

He shrugged. "I have no idea," he said. "You might just take a nap while Jeannine uses your body to communicate with us, or you might be along for the ride."

Jeannine hovered near Mary. "Are you sure you want to do this?" she asked. "We can try something else if you think it's too dangerous."

Mary shook her head. "I'm sure," she said. "Just don't make me do a chicken dance, okay?"

Jeannine chuckled. "I promise."

Chapter Sixteen

Bradley's cruiser rumbled down the snow-covered gravel road. The county plows had been through to push the snow into the ditches and sprinkle sand on the road for traction, but the roads were still slick.

"I'd always worry about losing an engine in one of the ditches in this kind of weather," Mike admitted. "Those big girls aren't made for slick narrow lanes."

"Yeah, during the last fire we had to call a couple snow plows and pull one of the hook and ladders out," Bradley replied. "Luckily it was after the fire was out, not before."

Mike looked out the window and sighed. "I miss working fires," he said. "It was such an adrenaline rush. From the moment that alarm sounded to the minute you finally put out the last flame, it was you against the fire. And you hoped you won that day."

"I heard you were one of the best they had," Bradley said.

"You were asking about me?"

Bradley shrugged. "Yeah, well, I had to know a little bit about the guy who could pop into Mary's life any time he wanted."

Mike laughed. "Yeah, anything you learned about me at the firehouse couldn't have eased your mind too much."

"Actually, other than being a lady killer, they all had great things to say about you," Bradley said.

Mike turned back to Bradley. "How are the guys doing?" he asked.

"Good," he said, nodding. "They're doing well. If you'd like, I could drive over there so you could check it out."

"Yeah, maybe after we check out the barn," he said. "That'd be nice. Thanks."

Bradley shrugged. "Just being nice so you keep your hands off my girl," he said.

Mike laughed. "I'd take her in a minute," he said. "But even though you act like an idiot, for some reason she's still in love with you."

Sighing deeply, he shook his head. "I know I don't deserve her and I don't know how I got so lucky," he said. "But I really do love her."

"Yeah, I know," he said. "I can tell."

The ruins of the barn came into view. "Whew, that used to be a great old barn," Mike said. "One of the few round barns left in the area."

"Yeah," Bradley said. "Once the hay caught on fire, there was nothing they could do to save it. The fire department had no idea anyone was inside. The owner had already cleared out the livestock before they got there."

"So, the body that you found," Mike said. "The person wasn't a family member?"

"No and there was no ID on the guy," he said. "So we're checking dental records. Hopefully that will give us something. Or…"

"Or his ghost is still here and willing to talk to us," Mike added.

"Yeah," Bradley said. "Exactly."

They pulled up in front of the barn; Bradley got out of his car and walked to it, Mike floating a few feet behind him. Within a few minutes, they heard the screen door on the nearby farmhouse close. Bradley looked up and saw the farmer, Leroy Johnson, heading toward him.

"Morning," Leroy said, extending his hand for a shake. "What brings you out here again?"

Bradley shrugged. "Just wanted to take another look around," he said. "Make sure I didn't miss anything,"

Leroy turned toward the barn and tipped back the brim of his baseball cap. "In all my years I never saw a barn go up like that. Strangest thing."

"What was strange?" Mike asked.

"What was strange?" Bradley repeated to Leroy.

"Barn door was open when I got out here," he said. "All the livestock were already in the pasture. Didn't lose any animals, not a one."

"That's strange for an arsonist," Mike said to Bradley. "They like to see things burn."

"The other farms that lost barns, did the same thing happen to them?" Bradley asked.

Leroy scratched the side of his head. "You know, now that you mention it, I think I remember some of them saying the same thing," he replied slowly. "That's a strange coincidence."

"That's not a coincidence," Mike said. "Something stinks here. Might be insurance fraud, might be something else. When there's fire, animals hide, they don't try to escape. That livestock was let out before the fires were started."

"So, in your experience, when there's a fire, do livestock try to escape?" Bradley asked Leroy.

Leroy shook his head. "Naw, they ain't smart enough to escape," he said. "They try to hide. Most livestock dies of smoke inhalation in barn fires. If they had tried to escape, they would have made it."

"So, do you think they're breeding smarter livestock?" Bradley asked.

Leroy laughed. "Only if they've graduated from damn stupid to just plain stupid," he said.

Bradley chuckled. "Thanks, Leroy. Hey, you don't mind if I walk around a little?"

"Naw, enjoy yourself, take your time," he said. "If you need something, I'll be in the machine shed."

Once Leroy was out of hearing distance, Bradley turned to Mike. "What do you think?"

Mike was already walking through the remains of the barn, examining the scorched pieces of wood and the debris on the ground. "The fire started here," he said, "in the center of the barn. Where did you find the body?"

Bradley picked his way through the rubble and joined him. "Back here," he said, pointing to an area a few yards away from them. "He was covered by an old metal trough. It was the only thing that kept him from being cremated."

"Did you ask where that trough used to be?" Mike asked.

Bradley nodded. "Yeah, Leroy had it up in the loft," he said. "Didn't use it anymore, but didn't want to throw it away in case he needed it."

Mike studied what remained of the support beams and loft of the barn. "My guess would be the fire spread up first, instead of out," he said slowly, pointing to the scorch lines on the beams. "The loft caught and the floor panels were weakened, so the trough fell through the floor on top of the body. But whoever was there was dead before the fire started."

"So, you think the fire was set to cover up a murder?" Bradley asked.

Mike nodded. "Yeah, I'd put a month's salary on that one."

Bradley looked around the area. "You see any ghosts walking around out here?"

Mike shook his head. "Nope, and that makes my theory even stronger. That body wasn't killed here, he was brought here."

"Perfect crime, except the trough got in the way."

"Yep, pretty much how I see it."

"You wouldn't consider staying on this case with me?" Bradley asked as they made their way out of the wreckage and walked to the cruiser.

"Just try and take me off this case," Mike said.

"I was hoping you'd say that."

Chapter Seventeen

"Ian, are you sure you know what you're doing?" Stanley asked, watching as Mary lay on the couch and Jeannine hovered above her.

"No, Stanley, I haven't the damndest idea what I'm about to do here," he said. "But I'm doing what seems to be logical."

Mary patted Ian's arm. "We have confidence in you," she said. "Don't we, Jeannine?"

Jeannine chuckled. "Sure we do. Besides Hawaii is lovely this time of year."

"Oh, that's easy for you to say," Mary said. "You can float on clouds. I'd fall like a rock."

"You aren't going to Hawaii," Ian grumbled. "Now if you'd just give a man a moment of silence we could get things going here."

Mary bit back her laughter. "Sorry, I'll be quiet."

"Me too," Jeannine said. "Sorry, Dad."

They both burst into giggles.

"Oh, and it's a jolly time for everyone until someone gets possessed," Ian lectured.

The laughter continued for a few more minutes, then Mary took a deep breath, wiped her eyes and turned to Ian. "I do apologize," she said. "I get this way when I'm nervous."

Ian nodded. "Understood," he said. "But if you could both concentrate, I think I'm ready to try this."

Mary took another deep breath and nodded. The mood in the room changed as Mary closed her eyes and began the deep rhythmic breathing Ian had suggested.

"Aye, that's grand, Mary," he said. "Now, I want you to hold my hand. There you go. If things get a bit dicey for you, you know I'm here for you. Okay?"

Mary nodded.

"Now, Mary, do you give Jeannine's spirit permission to enter your body?" he asked.

Once again, Mary nodded. "Yes, yes I do."

"And Jeannine," Ian continued. "Do you promise to do no harm to Mary while you inhabit her body? And promise not to misuse the privilege Mary's granted you?"

"Yes, I promise," Jeannine said.

"Mary, I want you to picture yourself in a room, a cozy room, that's comfortable and friendly," he said. "Look around the room; it's filled with all of the things you love. There are photos of your family and friends, books you've read, movies you've watched and even your memories are stored in this room."

Mary smiled.

"Ah, that's fine now," Ian said. "Now, Mary, walk to the door of the room and let Jeannine inside to be with you."

Mary moved through her cozy room, all colored in gold, browns and deep reds. There were overstuffed leather chairs and brightly colored thick rugs. Chenille throws waited for snuggling and a blazing fire was within a stone hearth. She ran her hands along the leather bound books in the oak bookcases and caught the scent of a burning candle.

The door was oak and curved at the top. It had a brass handle and a small window framed in brass. She peeked through it and saw Jeannine waiting. She opened the door. "Jeannine, my friend, come in," she said.

Ian watched Jeannine's spirit float down into Mary's body.

"Did it work?" Rosie whispered.

Ian turned and nodded in Rosie's direction, then put his finger over his lips to remind her to remain quiet.

"Oh, that's right," she said, "I'm supposed to be quiet."

Stanley rolled his eyes. "Shhhhhh," he whispered harshly.

Ian grinned and turned back to Mary.

"Jeannine, if you can hear me, I want you to squeeze Mary's right hand."

He felt the light squeeze on his hand. "Excellent. Now I want you to listen to my voice and only my voice," he said. "You are in a safe place and your friend Mary is right there beside you. I want you to relax. Close your eyes and take deep cleansing breaths."

Mary's rhythmic breathing changed to deeper, fuller breaths.

"Aye, that's good, that's good," he said. "Now I want you to clear your mind and just think of the things I'm saying to you and nothing else."

"Mary, are you with me too?" he asked.

Mary nodded her head.

"Good. I want you to relax too," he said. "It's going to be like you're a passenger in a car. You will see what's going on, but you don't have to worry about driving. Just relax and watch, okay?"

She nodded again.

"Now Jeannine," Ian said. "I want you to go back in your memories. I want you to go back to the day you and Bradley went for the ultrasound."

Mary smiled and moved her left hand over her stomach. "A girl," she whispered. "Bradley, we're going to have a girl."

She laughed lightly. "No, you can't paint the nursery Bears blue, it has to be pink.

"Really, Bradley, I'm not an invalid. Women have babies all the time, all over the world," she sighed heavily. "Okay, fine, I promise."

"Now Jeannine," Ian said. "We're going forward to the next morning. Tell me about that day."

"It's a beautiful day outside," she said. "The sun is shining, the grass is green and I'm going to have a baby girl. Bradley made me breakfast in bed. Not only is he going to spoil me, he's going to make me fat. He must think I'm giving birth to a small horse."

She giggled.

"Okay, he's gone to work," she said. "Good thing, because he doesn't know my secret."

Rosie and Stanley sat up in their chairs and looked at Mary.

"What secret?" Ian asked.

She giggled. "He's been so worried about me and the baby, he forgot his birthday was next week," she whispered. "I'm having Harvey Wasserman help me put together a man cave for him down in the basement. Harvey knows everything about computers there is to know and he is building a computer just for Bradley. Bradley's going to be so surprised."

"When does Harvey come by?" Ian asked.

"After Mercedes, his wife, goes to the gym," she said. "Mercedes can't keep a secret."

"So, Bradley just left," Ian said. "Let's go back there."

"Okay, he kissed me goodbye," she sighed. "It was a really good kiss…"

Mary stood at the bottom of the stairs. She looked around and realized she was in Bradley's house. Bradley was on the stairs, adjusting his tie as he carelessly jogged down. He kissed her on the cheek as he passed, then walked over to the mirror on the wall to check his tie. She walked up behind him and nearly choked when she saw Jeannine standing where she should be. She was inside Jeannine, living her memories. How the hell did that happen?

Bradley moved past her and opened the closet by the door. She watched him unlock the small safe

123

against the wall and retrieve his gun. He checked the safety, placed the gun in his holster and closed the closet door.

"Now, you remember what you promised," he said, walking back to her.

"No heavy lifting, no heavy cleaning and no heavy breathing," she said with a grin.

He pulled her into his arms. "I'll give you heavy breathing," he whispered just before he crushed her lips with his.

Her already hyper-active hormones soared into high gear. She wrapped her arms around him and held as tightly as she could. "Let's go back upstairs, darling," she whispered against his mouth. "You can be a little late."

Okay, this could get a little awkward.

He put his hands on her shoulders and eased her away. "Do you want me to lose my job?" he asked.

She nodded. "Yes, because then you could stay home and be my sex slave."

His deep laugh did nothing to ease her desire. "There is nothing I would want more than to stay home with you, Jeannine," he said. "But I've got to go and make the world a safer place for mankind."

Mary pouted for a moment, but he kissed her again and patted her on the bottom. "Stay out of trouble."

"I will," she said. "I love you."

"I love you too."

She watched him pull his car out of the driveway. He waved to her as he drove down the street.

"Okay, Jeannine, what happened next?" Ian asked.

She paused for a moment. "Oh, I realized it was trash day," she said. "So I went out to the garage and started to pull the garbage can out to the curb."

"Started to pull?" Ian asked. "Did something stop you?"

"Yes," she said. "Mr. Turner, our neighbor stopped me. He grabbed hold of both of my hands and pulled them off the garbage can."

"What did he do next?"

"He told me Bradley warned him that I might try to do some heavy lifting and he promised Bradley he would watch out for me," she said. "I explained that rolling a wheeled trash can from the garage to the curb really did not constitute heavy lifting. But he wouldn't let me do it. He just pulled it down the driveway himself."

Mary watched the middle-aged man with the thinning comb-over and slight muffin-top wheel the garbage can to the curb. He pulled a white handkerchief from his pocket and patted his top lip and forehead. "A little warm out here today, isn't it?" he called.

Mary smiled and nodded. "Yes, it is," she said. "I hope it cools off."

He walked back up the driveway and stood in front of her.

"Yes siree, sure is hot out here. A man could sure work up a thirst."

Mary smiled. "Would you like to come in for some fresh lemonade, Mr. Turner?" she asked.

"Now how many times have I asked you to call me Bob?" he said.

She smiled at him. "Bob, would you like a glass of lemonade?"

"That would be a fine treat."

They walked into the house and Mary led the way to the kitchen. "I made some cookies yesterday," she said, as she poured him a tall glass of lemonade. "I know it's early, but they are oatmeal raisin, so they're like a breakfast food."

"Well, can't see that a couple of cookies would hurt," he said as he sucked in his abdomen. "Sweets don't faze this body. Built rock solid. It's the genes."

"You are so lucky," she replied, biting back a smile.

She turned and took another glass out of the cupboard in order to take a moment and school her features. Pouring herself a glass of lemonade gave her another few moments to gain her composure.

When she turned, she was surprised to find Bob right behind her. She jumped back, but found herself pressed against the counter. "Can I help you?" she asked.

Bob stepped back and blushed. "I was just taking another couple of cookies," he said. "I wanted to get them before you turned around."

126

She smiled, but moved away so there was plenty of space between them. "I have plenty. Would you like me to put a dozen in a plastic bag for you?"

Bob nodded and smiled. "That would be great."

"How long did your neighbor stay?" Ian asked.

"Just a few minutes and then he left, with a dozen cookies in a bag, and a half dozen more in his hands," she laughed. "He is such an odd man."

"Odd in what way?" Ian asked.

She shrugged. "Well, he keeps to himself. Never has anyone over to visit. He even works from his home. No one knows what he does. He's just odd."

"But he came into your house," Ian reminded her.

She nodded. "Yeah, he comes over quite a bit," she said. "I think he's just lonely."

"Okay, Jeannine, what happens next?"

"Bob left and Harvey brought some more boxes over and put them in the basement," she said and giggled. "Poor Bradley, every time he heads toward the basement door I pretend I get a cramp and he rushes over to take care of me. He hasn't been down there in weeks."

"What other things do you keep down there?" he asked.

"You know, house control stuff," she replied. "The fuse box, the water heater, the furnace, the alarm system controls, the vacuum cleaning system…"

"The alarm system controls?" Ian asked. "Do you use your alarm system?"

She shook her head. "Yeah, the house is armed pretty much all the time," she said. "I think being a police officer makes you paranoid. I have to press a code every time I want to open a door."

"Did Harvey stay for very long?"

Mary watched a tall thin man scramble up the driveway balancing a number of assorted boxes. "Wait until you see what came today," he said to Jeannine. "The mother board, the thousand gig hard drive, the extra video cards, the core extreme processor and the 12GB2 Tri-Channel DDR3 SDRAM."

"Those are good things?" she asked.

"Only if you want CPUs pushed up almost 4 giga-hertz, that's like two or three additional bin speeds and the highest overclocked speeds available in the gaming industry, as well as being able to power up like three more independent digital displays all while increasing the gaming speed to 100 percent," he responded.

Jeannine nodded. "And you want that, right?"

"Oh, yeah, you want that real bad," he said.

She held the door open and he hurried inside. "I can't stay too long," he said. "Mercedes was complaining about cramping, so I don't think she's going to stay at the gym for long. So I'll just put these downstairs and then head out."

"Okay, that's great," she replied. "Thanks again, Harvey, for doing this. Bradley is going to be thrilled."

"Hey, it's a blast being able to put it together for him," he said with a grin. "The only condition is that I get to play with it occasionally."

"I'm sure Bradley will be happy to share," she said, praying that Bradley indeed be willing to share.

Jeannine opened the door for Harvey and he went downstairs. She heard the washing machine alarm go off and hurried back to the laundry room to switch the clothes from the washer to the dryer.

Taking the dry clothes out, she took the time to fold them and put them in piles. A few minutes later she walked into the kitchen and was surprised to find Harvey rustling through her cabinets.

"Are you looking for something?" she asked.

Harvey turned around quickly, guilt written across his face. "I guess you caught me," he said.

"Caught you doing what?"

"Searching for cookies," he admitted. "Mercedes has us on some crazy high grain, low-fat diet, and I don't think I'm going to make it. I saw Bob carrying out some cookies..."

Jeannine lifted the front of the bread box and pulled out the container of cookies. She popped open the top and slid them across the counter. "Help yourself," she said.

Harvey slipped one into his mouth and stuffed a couple more into his pockets. "Thanks," he mumbled around the mouth filled with cookie. "Thanks a lot."

Jeannine laughed as she watched him jog back down the street to his house, stuffing himself with the cookies along the way.

"He only stayed to put some boxes in the basement and eat some cookies," Jeannine said with a chuckle. "Quite a few cookies."

"Sounds like you had a busy morning," Ian remarked. "Did anyone else come by?"

"Yes, Gary stopped by for a few minutes to return some tools he borrowed from Bradley, she said. "We chatted for a couple of minutes in the kitchen and then he had to hurry to his morning appointments."

"Anyone else?"

The smile left Jeannine's face and she began to apply pressure to Ian's hand. "Mercedes," she whispered. "Mercedes came by with the muffins."

Chapter Eighteen

Bradley pulled the cruiser into the large front drive of the station house, far enough to the side that if the firemen had to leave in a hurry, he would not be in the way. He walked up to the station door and glanced behind him to see Mike following slowly, hesitantly.

"You okay?" he asked.

Mike nodded. "Yeah, it's just a little strange to be back here," he said. "It's a little sobering to see that life does go on without you."

"Life might go on, because it has to," Bradley replied. "But never doubt that you were missed. You can't replace a good man like you, Mike."

"Aw, Chief, you're going to make me blush," Mike said, and then he stopped and met Bradley's eyes. "Actually, I appreciate it. I really do."

Bradley shrugged. "Hey, no big deal," he said. "It's the truth."

Bradley entered the station and immediately met by Jack Williamson, the fire chief. "Chief," Jack said with a smile.

"Chief," Bradley replied with a grin, shaking hands with the old fireman. Jack had worked his way up the ranks and was probably near retirement, but he had the best investigative skills in the department and no one, including Jack, wanted to see him out of the firehouse.

"So, what's up?" Jack asked.

"I took a little trip back to Leroy's place," Bradley explained. "Things just don't seem to be adding up, so I wanted to get your take on it. Got a few minutes?"

"Sure, as long as the alarm stays quiet," he said.

They walked into one of the rooms off the main room that held the fire trucks and the equipment. It was about the size of Bradley's office, which wasn't saying much for it. It had just enough room for a desk, a file cabinet, a couple of chairs and a folding table that held a coffee maker and an assortment of mugs. "Want a cup?" Jack offered.

"No, I'm good," Bradley said, taking a seat across from the desk. "What do you think about those barn fires, Jack?"

"I think either we got ourselves one of those animal activists who thinks animals ought to be allowed to run free in the fields and not be warm and dry in a barn, or we got ourselves someone who's burning down barns, but doesn't want the farmers to suffer too much."

"Yeah, someone who feels like he has to burn down the barns, but takes the trouble to get anything of value out of them first," Bradley agreed.

Jack nodded. "And, I gotta say, usually those activist folks like to advertise what they're doing. So my money's on the second guess."

Bradley sat back in the chair. "You heard we found a body in the last barn," he said.

Jack nodded. "Yeah, I figured it was some drifter that took a nap in the wrong barn."

"Yeah, except the guy was dead before he got to the barn," Bradley said.

Jack's eyebrows rose. "You don't say. Well, that adds a little twist to the second scenario. Someone burning down a bunch of barns, so one more won't be looked at too closely."

"Yeah, and if the fire hadn't burned upwards first into the rafters and dropped an old metal trough on top of our victim, the plan would have probably worked."

Jack rubbed his chin with his hand. "So, you got anyone missing?"

"Checking that out," Bradley said. "And we're checking dental records. Hopefully we'll get an ID on our John Doe."

Jack leaned forward. "Got to tell you, Bradley, those fires were set by someone who knew what they were doing. Just enough damage, but not too much. No chance of spreading over to the farmhouses. No chance of hopping to another building."

"Who called them in?"

Jack chuckled. "Funny, I was just wondering that myself," he said. "I'll call over to 911 and get that information. When you find out about that victim, you let me know, okay?"

Bradley stood and shook hands with Jack. "Yeah, I'll keep you in the loop."

Jack moved around his desk slowly, his joints reacting to the cold weather, and put his hand on Bradley's shoulder. "I never got to thank you for solving the case involving Mike Richards. He was a good guy and one of the best firemen I'd ever known."

"Well, thanks, but I didn't do the solving," he replied. "Mary O'Reilly solved it and saved my life while she was doing it."

Jack looked at him from the corner of his eye. "Isn't she that kook who believes in ghosts?"

An empty mug slid across the card table and flew into the wall.

Jack stared at the shattered remains of the cup for a moment and then, eyes wide, turned back to Bradley.

Bradley smiled. "Yeah, that would be the one," he said. "See ya around, Jack."

Mike followed Bradley out of the room. "Just when I'm getting teary eyed listening to how much he likes me, he has to go and call Mary names," Mike said. "What a jerk."

Bradley chuckled. "Yeah, he might just be rethinking his position on ghosts after your little crockery missile."

"I always hated that cup anyway," Mike said.

"Hey, Bradley, hold on for a minute," Jack called from the office.

Bradley turned.

"You talking to me?" Mike said, turning with Bradley. "You talking to me?"

Bradley rolled his eyes at Mike. "Yeah, Jack, what do you need?"

Jack walked forward. "You saw that, right?" he asked. "You saw that cup fly off the table."

Bradley folded his arms over his chest and met Jack's eyes. "Yeah, I saw it."

"So, if it was like, an earthquake, all of the cups would have flown off the table, right?"

Bradley nodded. "Yep, that would make sense."

"So, what caused it?"

Bradley lifted one hand and stroked his chin, mirroring Jack's movement earlier. "Well, it could be the bottom of that glass was wet, so it slid across the table in its own. Could be the porcelain in that particular cup was heated so it would be sensitive to certain sound waves and we just had a sonic boom over Freeport. Or it could be Mike Richards got pissed because you called his good friend, and the woman who solved his murder, a kook."

Jack's mouth dropped open.

"By the way, Mike says he never liked that cup anyway," Bradley finished and then turned and walked out of the firehouse with Mike floating close behind.

"Okay, even I have to admit, that was great," he said. "Poor Jack, he's going to be walking around the station worried that I'm going to jump out and scare him."

Bradley chuckled. "Serves him right. Thanks for standing up for my girl, Mike."

"Our girl," Mike said.

"Our girl," Bradley agreed.

Chapter Nineteen

"No, dear, I came by with the muffins," Rosie said. "Me…Rosie."

"Shhhhhh," Stanley said. "She ain't thinking about this morning, she's thinking about eight years ago."

"She can remember having muffins eight years ago?" she said in amazement. "Well, then, she doesn't need to be hypnotized at all. She has an amazing memory."

"Listen, Rosie, she don't remember it at all," he whispered urgently. "It's the hypnosis; it's walking her through the day she disappeared. Remember when she was worried about your muffins this morning? That's because something bad happened with muffins on the day she got took."

"Well, I know a bad muffin can stay with you for a long time," Rosie agreed. "Especially a bran muffin. Oh, those can be the worst."

Ian looked over his shoulder at Rosie and Stanley, shot them a stern look and put his finger back over his lips.

"That's right," Rosie whispered. "We are supposed to be quiet. Stanley, stop making noise."

Stanley rolled his eyes and refrained from saying a word.

"Jeannine," Ian said. "Jeannine, you don't have to worry. Remember, I'm here with you. Nothing can hurt you. Now tell me about Mercedes."

"I was in the kitchen and I finally got to drink some of the lemonade I poured when Bob came over," she explained. "I realized I had to go to the bathroom. You always have to go to the bathroom when you're pregnant. I was walking toward the hall, when I heard someone at the door. I almost didn't go because it was Mercedes."

"Is there something wrong with Mercedes?"

"No, nothing at all. Well, except for being a nasty, gossiping, mean and spiteful…woman," Jeannine said.

"I don't think she meant to say woman, Stanley," Rosie whispered.

Stanley turned to her with his finger over his lips. "Hush."

"So, you answered the door," Ian said. "Then what happened."

"She came in with one of her fancy baskets filled with the most disgusting muffins I've ever had the misfortune of tasting," she said. "The only way I was able to swallow it was by gagging down the last sips of lemonade."

"Then what happened?" Ian asked.

Jeannine paused and Mary's face turned pale. "I…I got sick," she said hesitantly. "I felt really dizzy, like I was going to faint."

"Did Mercedes help you?"

Jeannine shook her head. "No, no, I made her leave. I didn't want her in the house if I was going to be sick."

"What did you do next?"

"I needed Bradley," she said, her voice weaker. "I was so frightened. I was worried about the baby. I needed Bradley."

"What did you do?"

"My phone. My phone is in the living room," she said. "I have to get my phone and call Bradley."

She stopped talking and took some gasps of air.

"Jeannine, where are you?"

"I'm in the hall, I can barely walk. I feel so dizzy. Holding on to furniture and walls, have to make it to the couch for my phone. Finally, I'm there. But, I can't see the numbers. Everything is so blurry. I feel so sick. Maybe if I just rest. If I just close my eyes."

Mary was still, her face was white and her breathing shallow.

"Jeannine?" Ian asked urgently. "Jeannine, are you still there?"

Mary looked around the room. This was not where she was supposed to be. It was dark and damp and smelled like dirt.

"Hello," she called out. "Is anybody there? I need help."

Her vision still hadn't recovered from earlier, everything was blurry. She tried to sit up, but her legs wouldn't hold and she fell back against the

139

cushions of an old couch. Something stirred in the corner of the room. Leaning forward she squinted her eyes to try and focus on it.

"No, no, no," Jeannine screamed, squeezing Ian's hand. "He touching me, he's touching me. Make him go away."

"Jeannine, take a deep breath. You're fine, you're safe," Ian said. "He can't hurt you."

Mary shivered with disgust as the man's hand roamed freely over her body. She tried fighting him, but he easily captured both of her wrists in one hand. "Just a few more moments, darling," he whispered, "and the drugs will make you relax and then we can both enjoy ourselves."

"No, don't touch me," Mary cried. "I don't want you to touch me."

"Oh, darling, yes you do," he insisted. "You've always wanted me. You never wanted Bradley. I could tell by the way you looked at me. It was always me."

Tears flowed down Mary's cheeks as she fought for her freedom, but she could feel her consciousness slipping away. "That's right, my dear," he whispered, kissing her on the neck. "Relax and enjoy. You're going to love this."

Jeannine screamed and thrashed around on the couch. "No, you are not going to touch me. Stop it!! Stop it!!"

"Bring her out of it," Stanley yelled, storming across the room. "Bring her out of it now."

Ian placed his hands on Mary's shoulders. "Jeannine, it's Ian," he shouted. "Jeannine, listen to me. I want to help you, but you have to do what I say."

She whimpered, but calmed down. "Help me," she cried.

"Jeannine, look around for the door you came in through," he said. "The door in Mary's room. Can you see it?"

"It's dark in here," she said. "I can't see it."

"Look around," Ian insisted. "It's right there, behind you."

"Oh, I see it. I see it," she cried.

"Good, good girl," he said. "Now go to the door and open it up. Once through, you will be safe."

Ian released his breath in relief once he saw Jeannine appear above Mary. But, his relief was short-lived when he saw that Mary had not responded to the hypnotic suggestion. "Mary," Ian said, squeezing her hand. "Mary, can you hear me?"

Mary moaned softly and shook her head.

"Mary, where are you?" he asked.

"Well, it sure in hell isn't Hawaii," she responded. "Ian bring me home."

Ian took a deep breath and wiped a tear from his cheek. "You certainly know how to age a man, Mary," he said. "Can you see the room you started in? The room with your books and memories?"

She shook her head. "No, I'm in this dark place and it's really creepy in here. I was here with Jeannine, but now I'm just here on my own."

"Well, then," Ian said. "You get to use your skills, not Jeannine's. Mary, you're not the victim, you are the law enforcement officer. You can get out of that room."

Mary looked around the dark chamber. There was a wooden door at one end. She stood and felt more solid on her feet. She was a cop, a Chicago cop, no one pushed her around. She walked to the door and tried to pull it open, but it was locked.

"Ian, the door's locked," she said.

Ian knew that Mary's subconscious had to conquer the fear that was keeping her locked in Jeannine's memories. "Mary, kick the bloody hell out of the door," he said.

Mary backed up a few steps, raised her right leg and kicked through the center of the door. Light flooded in from the other side. She moved closer and kicked again. There was now a hole large enough for her to climb through.

"I see my room, Ian," she called.

"Good girl," he said. "Go to your room and lay down on the couch. I'll wake you up when Rosie has lunch ready for you."

He waited for a few minutes. "Mary, can you hear me?" he asked.

She nodded slowly.

"Mary, it's time to wake up now," he said.

Mary slowly opened her eyes and looked around. She sat up on the couch and stared at Ian for a moment. "How long was I gone?" she asked.

"Oh, well, you and Jeannine have been traveling in her memories for about an hour," he said. "Do you remember?"

She nodded. "Yes, I remember it all. I was there, Ian. I was living her memories."

"Well, that'll be a help to find the bastard who did this to her."

Mary shuddered. "Yes, and we'll send him to the same kind of hell he put her through."

Rosie and Stanley hurried over to Mary's side. "Mary, how do you feel?" Rosie asked.

"Like I've been beaten up," Mary said.

"Well, that's it," Stanley said. "That's the last time we let you do something damn foolish like that again. Hypnosis, bah, nothing but playing with folks' minds."

"Stanley," Mary said. "I have to do it again. We need to discover what happened to Jeannine. This time we only scratched the surface."

"Mary, dear, is there anything I can do for you?" Rosie asked.

Mary nodded. "For some reason, I thought you were making lunch."

Chapter Twenty

"I've searched this file three times and there are no crime scene photos that contain a basket of muffins on your kitchen counter," Mary said.

Mary, Ian, Rosie and Stanley were seated around the kitchen table munching on sandwiches, chips and homemade cookies, while they searched through boxes of information Bradley had gathered during his investigation.

"Does that matter?" Stanley asked. "Sounds like those muffins were a crime by themselves."

"Well, the only reason it matters is because Mercedes and her muffins were the last thing Jeannine remembers before she was taken," Mary said. "She remembers Mercedes leaving the house and the basket still on the counter. So, if they're not there, someone had to take them."

"But why would someone take the basket of muffins?" Rosie asked. "Could the kidnapper have been hungry?"

"Not for those muffins," Jeannine said.

"The muffins could have contained drugs and the kidnapper might not have wanted them around for evidence," Ian said.

"Which would mean that Mercedes had something to do with the kidnapping," Mary added.

"She could have just wanted her basket back," Jeannine said. "She brought them over in one of those fancy Longaberger baskets. Those are pretty expensive."

"But how did she get back in the house?" Mary asked. "And what did she see when she got here?"

Mary picked up her cell phone and pressed a speed dial number. "Hi," she said into the phone, her voice softening. "How was your day?"

"She's speaking with Bradley," Rosie said. "You can tell by the way she's smiling."

Mary grinned. "I'm putting you on speaker, so I won't be accused of neglecting my duty."

His laughter was broadcast across the room as Mary laid her phone on the table. "We had a couple of questions for you," she said.

"Okay, ask away," he said. "I've studied those case files so many times, I've probably memorized them."

"This might sound silly, but did you remember seeing a basket of muffins on the kitchen counter on the day of the break-in?" Mary asked.

"No," he replied slowly. "And, you know, now that you mention it. I always thought there was something wrong with the kitchen photos. Something I couldn't put my finger on. Do you have those photos in front of you?"

Mary pulled out the photos and placed them on the table.

"Well, it ain't what's in the photo," Stanley said. "It's what ain't in the photo. Look at the big clear spot on the counter there. There's crap scattered all over every other space in that kitchen, 'cepting for that one bare spot on the counter."

Mary examined the photo and realized that Stanley was right. "Stanley, you are a genius," she said. "He's right, Bradley. There's a bare spot on the corner, like someone…"

"Lifted a basket of muffins off the countertop," Bradley finished. "Damn, how could I have missed that after all these years?"

"You was looking at what was there, not what was missing," Stanley said. "Besides, why would you think to look at that bare spot? Don't beat yourself up, not everyone can be a genius like me."

Bradley chuckled. "Thanks Stan, I appreciate it. So, what's your next move?"

"Well, Mercedes is definitely on our list of possible suspects," Ian said, writing down her name on a yellow pad. "And it will be interesting to see if she still has her basket."

"Yeah, I think we'll pay her a visit tomorrow," Mary said. "Bradley, we're going to keep going on here for a while. Thanks for your help."

"I need to tell all of you how grateful I am for your work on this case," Bradley said. "You've gotten further in two days than I got in eight years."

"Well, it's easy when Mary is so willing…" Rosie said, but was cut off when Stanley's hand came over her mouth.

"Mary is so willing to do what?" Bradley asked, suspicion in his voice.

Stanley sent Rosie a warning look.

"Oh, so willing to let us take cookie breaks whenever we want to," Rosie said. "I swear I'm going to gain ten pounds working on this case."

"Rosie, begging your pardon, but you're the worst liar I've ever heard," Bradley said. "Mary, remember what I told you before you left. Don't take unnecessary risks."

"Bradley, I haven't even left this house yet," she said. "Don't worry, we are being very careful."

"Ian?"

"Aye, she's telling the truth," he said. "Most of the day she's spent lying on the couch. Word of honor."

"Well, thank you, again," Bradley said. "Call me if you need anything else."

"We will," Mary said. "Good night Bradley."

"Good night."

Mary disconnected the call and then turned back to the group. "Well, I think that went well," she said. "Now, who else gets put on the suspect list?"

"I vote for Mercedes's husband, Harvey, the techie guy," Stanley said. "He wasn't anxious for his wife to find out he was visiting Jeannine and you can never trust those nerd types. Can't barely understand them half the time."

Ian nodded and added Harvey to the list.

"Oh, I want a turn," Rosie said. "Bob, the quiet unassuming neighbor, those are always the murderers in the made-for-television movies. I think Bob did it."

Ian shrugged. "Okay, I'm adding Bob."

"How about Gary?" Mary asked. "He was here that morning too."

"Aye, but Mary we've met Gary and the only reason he dropped by was to return some tools," Ian said. "And Bradley said he'd trust him with his life."

"We have to consider all the possibilities," Mary said, looking pointedly at Ian. "Add Gary."

Ian rolled his eyes. "Fine, I'll put him down."

"So, who else do you we want on the list?" Stanley asked.

Mary scanned the list Bradley had collected. "Well, actually, Bradley did a remarkable job of compiling and following through on any other suspect that wasn't a neighbor," she said. "So, let's start with these four and see if they lead us to anyone else."

"Okay, that makes sense," Ian said. "So, how do we divide up the names?"

"Oh, can I help?" Rosie asked. "I've been told I have a remarkable ability to relate to men."

"That's because they all fall in love with you, you goose," Stanley grumbled. "You ain't going to have a killer falling in love with you. It's too dangerous."

Rosie giggled and patted her hair. "Stanley, that's not true," she said, with a titter. "Perhaps they develop a crush on me, but I can't say they fall in love."

"Listen, girlie," Stanley said. "You ain't going out there looking for some killer all by yourself. It ain't safe and you ain't trained for it."

He looked over at Mary. "You tell her, she ain't going out there," he said.

Mary nodded and turned to Rosie. "Stanley's right. This could be dangerous and I don't want to risk your life," she said, and then turning to Stanley, "either of your lives. However, I do need your help, so we will plan a way to allow you to do that, without endangering your well-being."

"So what's your plan?" Stanley asked.

Mary turned and smiled at Rosie. "So, Rosie, how do you feel about making some cookies?" she asked. "A lot of cookies."

"I can do that. Why?"

Ian nodded and smiled. "Because we are going to go visiting our new neighbors with plates of cookies," he said. "Aren't we Mary?"

"Yes we are," she replied. "We'll team up and meet the neighbors in pairs. Stanley and Rosie, I want you to go next door and meet Bob."

"Bob? You want us to meet with Bob?" Stanley asked. "Don't you think that's a little dangerous for Rosie?"

"I wouldn't send you into any situation that I thought was going to be dangerous," Mary said. "And I don't want you to say anything or do anything that will make Bob nervous or feel threatened. All I want you and Rosie to do is go over there and act like his friendly new neighbors, that's it."

"That's it? That's all you want us to do?" Stanley asked with disgust. "Visit and eat cookies."

Ian nodded. "And place a small, indiscreet bugging device in his home."

Stanley grinned. "Now you're talking."

Chapter Twenty-one

"So how's Mary?" Mike asked once Bradley hung up.

Bradley stared at the phone in his hand. "Mary's taking some kind of risk they don't want to tell me about."

Mike snorted. "Well, that's unusual."

"What does that mean?" he asked.

"Mary is a perfectly capable, trained law enforcement professional," Mike said. "You want to protect her and treat her like…"

"Like what?" Bradley asked.

"Like a girl," Mike said.

"Well, damn it, she is a girl."

"No, she's a woman and a damn sexy one too," Mike said, laughing out loud when Bradley glared at him. "And I understand your instinctive desire to protect the people you love. But that is just what Mary is doing too. She knows you worry, so she just leaves out the parts that would freak you out."

"I should never have let her take this case on," Bradley muttered.

Mike laughed even harder. "Yeah, because she's doing this because you let her," he said. "Wake up and smell the cookies, Chief. She's doing this because Jeannine came to her. You couldn't have stopped her."

Bradley dropped down onto the couch and leaned back, placing his hands over his face. "This is crazy. I'm crazy," he said. "I'm a control freak and I have absolutely no control over this woman. She is going to drive me to an early death."

Mike grinned. "Yeah, but the journey there will be a hell of a good time."

Bradley slipped his hands from his face, turned to Mike and smiled. "Yeah, it will be, won't it?"

"Damn straight!" Mike said. "So, since you can't do anything about it anyway, how about a distraction? Want to watch some TV?"

Bradley reached for the remote, but before he could put his hand on it, it flew through the room into Mike's hand. "Called it," he said with a grin.

"I thought this was supposed to distract me," Bradley complained.

"Oh, I promise," Mike said. "You will be distracted."

Mike clicked the remote, the television turned on and the program guide appeared on the screen. "You have two thousand channels," Mike said. "There's got to be something on that we both will agree on."

Mike clicked through the channels until he found one he liked. "I like this show," he said. "One of the most realistic crime shows on the tube."

He pressed the remote.

"I'm sorry, Jethro, she's dead. There was nothing we could do."

152

"I told her I'd protect her."

"She died in the line of duty, doing what she wanted to do."

Bradley looked over at Mike. "I don't think so," he said.

"Yeah, right!" Mike said, quickly changing the channel.

A popular ghost movie appeared on the screen. Mike turned to Bradley and grinned. "Bradley," he whispered slowly. "You see dead people."

"Try again," Bradley suggested.

Mike flipped through a few more channels.

"The Bears are at 2nd and goal. With only one minute on the clock, they could take this game. They only need three points to win and a touchdown would clinch the game.

They get into formation, the ball is snapped."

Mike and Bradley leaned toward the screen.

"The defense is coming on strong. The Quarterback is feeling a lot of pressure."

"Throw the ball," Mike urged. "Come on, there's a dozen guys open out there."

"The Quarterback steps out of the hole. He can't seem to find anyone to throw the ball."

"Where the hell is the offense, why isn't anyone protecting this guy?" Bradley yelled at the screen.

"He steps back and trips."

"He trips?" Mike yells, standing up and moving closer to the screen. "We pay him 1.2 million dollars and he trips?"

"The defense is rushing. Oh, no, they've got a hold of him. Is that the ball? Did the ball just pop loose from his hold?"

"Of course it did," Bradley yelled, joining Mike next to the TV. "Do you need glasses too?"

"The ball is loose and it's been picked up by one of the linebackers from the other team. And he's making a run for it. Look at him go. He's on the fifty, he's on the forty, he's on the thirty."

"Run after him, you idiots," Mike screamed, jumping up and down. "Grab him, jump on him, break his legs. Stop him!!"

Bradley turned to Mike. "Break his legs?"

"Well, they're not carrying guns," he pointed out.

"Good point," Bradley agreed.

"Touchdown!!! Well, folks, there is no way the Bears are going to be coming back from…"

Mike changed the channel. "I couldn't take the stress," Mike admitted.

"Good point."

"Welcome to America's Next Top Model."

"No way," Bradley said. "This is chick-TV."

"Yesterday we filmed on the shores of Hawaii. The contestants modeled swimsuits in the surf and sand."

A scene of twelve scantily clad models flashed on the screen.

"Whoa, wait just a second," Bradley said.

They both backed away from the television and, without taking their eyes off the screen, sat in their chairs.

"That little blonde is pretty cute," Mike said.

"Yeah, but doesn't that brunette kind of look like Mary," Bradley said. "Maybe a little taller and, you know…"

He arched his hands about a half foot in front of his chest. "She might be a little bigger…"

Mike cocked his head slightly. "Yeah, yeah, you're right, she's a little bigger," he said, and then he stopped. "You know, not that I looked or anything."

Bradley glared at Mike.

"Hey, I'm dead, not blind."

"Shhh," Bradley said. "They're doing the judging."

A few minutes later the phone rang. Bradley, his eyes still on the screen, absently answered it. "Yeah, Chief Alden here," he said.

He immediately stood and walked away from the television and over to his desk on the other side of the room. "Okay, you're sure," he said. "Any record?"

Mike turned away from the television to listen to Bradley's side of the conversation.

"Okay, I got it," he said. "Paul Taylor, former Freeport resident. Recently released on parole, convicted of manslaughter in the death of his wife and three children. How did they die?"

155

"Oh, shit," Mike muttered, instantly knowing what Paul Taylor's conviction had been.

It was the case he had recently mentioned to Mary. The man had killed his family to avoid child support payments and then set fire to the home. Mike had been one of the first responders and had burst into the little girl's room before the fire reached it. But, when he picked her up, he knew she was already gone. He had taken off his mask and seen the bruises around her little neck.

Bradley hung up the phone and turned to Mike. "Mike, I need to ask you," he said. "What do you know about Paul Taylor?"

"Gotta go, Chief," Mike said, fading away.

"Mike get back here," Bradley called to the empty room. "Well, damn!"

Chapter Twenty-two

He flipped the switch and the dark underground room was filled with light. Pushing the heavy door closed until he heard the metallic click of the latch sliding into place, he hurriedly slipped the steel bolt into place, locking himself in.

He exhaled slowly and wiped the sweat from his brow. It had been a long day and all he could think about was coming home and talking to her. After all these years, he still loved her. He hoped she knew that he looked forward to the next decade as much as he had the past. It had been harder, of course, but he knew that the time they had spent apart physically would be rewarded in the next life, when they could be together forever.

He walked over to the old stereo sitting on a gray metal desk in one corner of the room. He brushed the dust off the black plastic. He was a little ashamed he had allowed it to get into this condition. Opening one of the drawers, he pulled out a bottle of Windex and a roll of paper towels. Within a few minutes, the desk and stereo gleamed like new.

Smiling, he stood back and admired it. She would be pleased. She liked when things were all tidied up.

Opening another drawer, he looked through his collection of CDs. He needed to select the perfect one; she was a little fussy when it came to her music. There it was, soft and romantic. It would remind her of all the wonderful times they spent together. He pushed on the top of the CD player; the lid sprung open and he slipped the CD inside and immediately pressed the Pause button.

Another drawer held two ivory candles in crystal candlesticks and a box of matches. Arranging the candles on either side of the desk, he lit them and inhaled the sweet beeswax scent as they began to burn.

Perfect, just perfect.

He walked back across the room and turned off the light. He knew she preferred candlelight to the harsh fluorescent lights. She had once said that candlelight was more flattering to a woman's features. Of course, he knew that was ridiculous, she was perfect in his eyes. But, he wanted to be sure she was pleased when they finally got to see each other.

Walking back to the desk, he pressed the Play button and the soft sounds of "Make It With You" by Bread echoed in the small chamber. He picked up a steel folding chair and carried it with him to the other side of the room in front of an older model upright freezer. He played with the chair for a few moments, angling it perfectly and then he finally sat down.

Reaching forward, he grasped the stainless steel freezer handle and pulled it open. A rush of icy vapor escaped into the room and he sat back, waiting for it to clear. Then he smiled.

"Good evening, darling," he whispered. "You look beautiful tonight."

The frozen women's upper torso was wrapped in clear plastic and was leaning against the side of the freezer wall. Frost had grown on her cheeks and forehead, giving her a sparkling, almost festive appearance. Whatever hair she might have had, had become brittle and fallen down in small pieces inside the wrapping. Her eyes were open and staring sightlessly forward.

On the shelf above were her remaining limbs, wrapped carefully in plastic and pushed to the back of the freezer. Next to the limbs was a white box, nestled carefully against the side of the wall.

"You look like you could use a shawl," he said.

He stood up and took a plastic container from the top of the freezer. Opening it, he pulled out an ivory colored woolen shawl and laid it carefully over the shoulders of the corpse. "There, that's much better," he soothed. "Is that better?"

He started to put the container back, when he paused. "What?" he said. "Oh, of course, I can do that."

He reached into the container again and pulled out a smaller woolen shawl. It was pink and had fringe on all four sides. "She always looks so lovely when she wears this," he said.

He reached into the freezer for the small white box and carefully opened the lid. The tiny frozen baby was no more than ten inches long and still wrapped in a fetal position. Sliding his hands beneath the plastic that enveloped the baby, he slipped the shawl around its tiny form.

He sat down in the chair, the swaddled baby in his arms and he slowly rocked back and forth. "Now we can be a family again."

Chapter Twenty-three

Sun was peeking through the windows when Mary woke up the next day. She sat up, stretched and...SMELLED COOKIES. Snatching her robe from the end of the bed, she hurried down the stairs to the kitchen. Stanley and Ian were already perched next to the island, waiting for Rosie to move the cookies from the cookie sheet to the cooling rack. And they were both still in their pajamas too.

Stanley was wearing flannel pajamas that were blue with a subtle pinstripe and Ian was in sweat pants and nothing else.

"Rosie, darling, they don't have to cool," Ian said. "They're better hot."

"You'll burn your mouth if I let you eat them this way," Rosie scolded. "You have to wait."

Stanley scooted around the island and was making his way toward the mixing bowl. Rosie picked up a wooden spoon and slapped it on the counter. "You stick your fingers into my cookie dough and I'll slap your hand," she threatened.

While she was busy with Stanley, Ian reached over and grabbed a hot cookie from the cooling tray. "Ouch, ouch, ouch," he yelled, as he tossed the cookie back and forth between hands, trying to cool it down.

Rosie turned to him. "Ian, I told you to wait."

He popped the cookie into his mouth, bit down and smiled. "Oh, Rosie," he said through a mouthful of cookie, "the temptation was just too great."

Mary opened the drawer in the counter and pulled out a teaspoon. While Rosie was busy scolding Ian, she stepped forward and scooped some of the dough out with her spoon.

"Hey," Stanley yelled, "Mary just stole some cookie dough."

"Tattle-tale," Mary said, sticking her dough-covered tongue out at Stanley. "Besides, I used a spoon, not my finger."

"Mary, I thought you were the mature one here," Rosie said.

"Excuse me?" Stanley asked. "She's the mature one? I'm old enough to be her grandfather."

"And you have cookie dough under your fingernail," Mary said.

"Stanley!" Rosie chided.

"Busted!" Mary grinned.

Ian grinned over at Mary and motioned with his head toward the cooling rack. She nodded eagerly. He grabbed another cookie and tossed it across the room to her. She took a bite and closed her eyes in complete ecstasy. "Oh, Rosie, these are so good," she said.

"Better than sex?" Jeannine asked, appearing in the kitchen.

Mary grinned. "Well, they're better than sledding."

"What?" Ian asked.

Mary chuckled. "Never mind."

"Okay, all of you, out of the kitchen," Rosie stated firmly. "We can't go interview bad guys if you are eating all of the cookies up. Go, go get dressed. Now!"

"Yes, ma'am," Ian said. "Stanley, do you want to use the shower first?"

Stanley nodded, "Yeah, then I get first dibs on the cooled cookies."

Mary walked over to the fridge and pulled out a Diet Pepsi. "Breakfast anyone?" she asked.

"You're as bad as Bradley," Jeannine said. "How can you drink that stuff?"

Ian poured himself a cup of tea. "Aye, I couldn't stomach it," he said. "Rosie, tell her she shouldn't be drinking that in the morning."

"You just don't understand the finer things in life," Mary said. "Right Rosie?"

"Oh, no, dear, I think that stuff is going to lead you to an early grave," she said, popping a cookie into her mouth. "Of course, so is this."

Ian grabbed another cookie and bit down. "Aye, but this is a lovely way to go."

"Why thank you dear," Rosie said. "Mary, will you listen for the timer? I'm going to run upstairs and get dressed."

"No, problem," Mary replied. "Take your time."

Once Rosie left the room, Jeannine hovered over to the stove. "I miss this," she said, running her hand over the dials. "I used to love to bake."

"I didn't realize you cooked?" Mary said.

She shook her head. "Oh, no, I was really bad at cooking. But, I loved baking. Cookies, brownies, and cakes," she smiled. "I would bake during the day, and we'd go out and pawn it off on the neighbors in the evening. If Bradley ate half of what I made, he would have been as wide as he was tall."

"Your neighbors must have loved you," Ian said.

Darkness fell across Jeannine's face. "Obviously not all of them."

Mary nodded. "Yes, you're right."

"So, Rosie mentioned you are visiting the bad guys today," Jeannine said. "Who are you going to see?"

Ian sat down at the table and pulled out the yellow pad with the names on them. "This is just to start," he said. "We'll see if they lead us to any more leads."

Mary joined him at the table, "We thought we'd start with the people you had contact with on that last day," she said. "Do you have any insight you can add?"

"Mercedes had a huge ego," she said. "And she is very susceptible to flattery."

She turned to Ian. "Especially from hunky men."

Ian grinned. "Well, I'll be sure to turn on the charm."

"We're going to be placing discreet bugging devices in their homes," Mary said. "Any suggestion where we should place it in Mercedes's house?"

"Probably her office," Jeannine suggested. "She spends most of her time there. And it seems to be the room she and Harvey use when they are having private discussions."

"So, how do we get her to show us her office?" Ian asked.

Jeannine smiled. "Ask her about her real estate awards," she said. "She has them mounted on the walls in her office."

"Perfect," Mary said.

"Jeannine, I want to have another session with you and Mary," Ian said.

Jeannine slid to the corner of the room. "It wasn't easy to be back there, Ian," she said. "I don't know…"

"I know it was hard," Mary said. "Somehow I lived through all the memories you were experiencing. I felt them too."

Jeannine moved closer to them. "You felt them?" she asked.

Mary nodded and closed her eyes for a moment. "His hands on my skin, his voice through the drugs, the cold and damp room and just the fear for the life of the baby," Mary said. "Yes I felt it all."

"So, when I remembered what happened, I wasn't alone," she said. "You were there with me."

"The whole time," Mary said.

"Do you want to do it again?" she asked. "Do you really want to go back there again?"

Mary took a deep breath and shook her head. "No, I don't. But I will, because I want to find out who did this to you," she said. "And I really want to kick his butt."

Jeannine giggled. "I wish I was more like you, Mary," she said. "I've never been very brave. I always ran away, instead of staying and fighting. I wonder…"

Mary stood and walked over to Jeannine. "You were brave," she said. "You put up with everything that happened to you because you were protecting your baby. You were amazing."

Jeannine turned to Ian. "We can do it again," she said. "Mary and me, we're going to kick some butt."

Ian nodded. "Aye, I can see that," he said. "Thank you, Jeannine."

Jeannine started to fade away. "No, thank you. Both of you."

Chapter Twenty-four

"So, how do I look?" Rosie asked, as she came down the stairs wearing a pink bouclé suit with a multi-colored scarf draped over her shoulders.

"You look lovely," Mary said.

"Why the hell you all dressed up like a frothy pink confection for some crazy killer?" Stanley asked. "You go back upstairs and dress in something less…less… Well, damn it, woman, you know what I mean."

Rosie stopped at the bottom of the stairs and put her hands on her hips. "No, Stanley, I don't believe I do understand what you mean," she said. "And I don't believe I'm going to change my clothes. I like being a pink confection."

Stanley walked across the room and stood in front of her. "I say you're going back up and getting yourself dowdied up," he said. "Ian, tell her."

Ian grinned and shook his head. "I'd say she should go out there just the way she is," he said. "All of her beauty is bound to distract the man. And when you add those cookies to the mixture… Well, you'll have no problem placing the bug in that house."

Rosie giggled softly. "Thank you, Ian," she said, slipping into her coat and picking up the plate of cookies. "Are you ready to go, Stanley?"

Stanley took Rosie's arm and placed it firmly around his. "You stay close to me, girlie, understand?" he said.

Rosie smiled up at him. "Of course, Stanley," she replied, scooting closer to him. "I'll stay as close as I can."

"Well, er, good," Stanley murmured, reaching up and loosening his collar a little. "Just so you know who's in charge."

Rosie laid her cheek against his shoulder for a moment. "Oh, Stanley, I know who's in charge."

Once the door closed behind them, Ian turned to Mary.

"And why do you think they call women the weaker sex?" he asked.

"A man wrote the book," Mary said with a shrug. "And his wife told him to put that in there."

Ian chuckled. "Well, poor Stanley," he said. "I don't believe he's realized yet that he's good and caught."

"Yeah, but I don't see him fighting his way loose," Mary said. "They're both pretty smitten."

Stanley helped Rosie down the slick driveway and on to the sidewalk. "Now, remember, we don't want to do anything to make Bob feel threatened," he said. "So, as far as he knows, we're just new neighbors."

"Yes, Stanley," she said. "And I'll distract him so you can put the bug somewhere in the house."

"Yeah, but don't take no chances," he said.

"I promise, Stanley."

168

They walked up the walk to Bob's house and climbed up the stairs to his front porch. Stanley rang the bell and then stood in front of the solid steel door that only had a peep hole, no window.

"Don't like people looking in," Stanley whispered to Rosie. "That ain't a good sign."

"Maybe he's shy," Rosie whispered back.

"Humph," Stanley said.

After a few moments they could hear the door being unlocked and then it was opened a crack. "Can I help you?" Bob asked curtly.

"Hello," Rosie said with a brilliant smile. "We're your new neighbors. We live just next door. I was baking this morning and thought I'd bring you over some cookies."

"Oh? New neighbors?" he said, widening the opening.

"Yes," she said. "We just moved in with our grandchildren. They're newlyweds, so we wanted to give them a little time alone. I'm sure you understand."

The door opened wider. "Moved in with grandchildren?"

Rosie moved in closer, thrusting the plate of cookies ahead of her. "Well, our granddaughter and her new husband," she said. "I'm Rosie and this is…"

Stanley moved forward and extended his head. "I'm Stanley, her husband," he said. "And you are?"

"Bob. Bob Turner," he said.

"Well, howdy, Bob," Stanley replied. "You don't mind if we come in for a moment or two? My Rosie here makes the best cookies in the whole state of Illinois."

"Um, no, come in," he said. "Come in."

Stanley put his arm around Rosie's shoulders and guided her into the small foyer.

Rosie swallowed a gasp and forced herself to smile at Bob. "Well, it seems you are a collector," she said as she looked around house.

Almost every inch of space was covered with stacks of newspapers and magazines, towers of boxes and piles of clothing. The furniture was covered, the floors were covered, the bookcases were covered and even the bathroom was filled. There were little pathways, just wide enough for one person to walk down, throughout the house.

Rosie and Stanley both jumped when they heard the distinct click of a steel bolt into a lock. They turned to see Bob locking them securely into the house. "You can't be too careful," Bob said. "Scary things have happened in this neighborhood."

"No, really?" Stanley responded. "This seems like such a nice neighborhood."

"Oh, about eight years ago," Bob responded. "The woman next door disappeared."

He looked at Rosie and smiled. "I'm sure you wouldn't want that to happen to your wife, would you?"

Stanley pulled Rosie a little closer. "No, I sure wouldn't," he said. "Course, nothing like that would happen while I was around."

Bob shook his head. "Good man," he said. "Protecting your wife should be the first priority in your life. Too many men think about themselves first."

Rosie swallowed and refreshed the smile on her face. "Where would you like me to put these cookies?" she asked. "In the kitchen?"

Bob pondered the question for a moment. "No, no, why don't we all go to my office?" he said. "Then we can sit, visit and get acquainted."

They followed him through a maze of garbage to the back of his house. Rosie almost screamed when a mouse darted from one stack across their path to another one, but Stanley placed his hand on her shoulder for reassurance. She turned and sent him a grateful smile. Stanley felt his heart hit the ground and then bounce right back up. *Well, dammit, I'm in love with her,* he suddenly realized.

As they passed through the house, Rosie's stomach clenched tighter and tighter. The house was filthy. She could see mouse droppings on most of the exposed surfaces, cobwebs hung everywhere and the air was filled with smell of mold. She shivered. *How does someone live like this?*

Bob finally led them to a door that was closed to the rest of the mess. He opened it and, unlike the rest of the house, Rosie could tell there was sunlight

171

streaming in from the windows. He entered the room first and motioned for them to follow.

The room was spotlessly clean, with a small desk and chair in one corner and a floral love seat, occasional chair and small coffee table in the other corner. Rosie couldn't believe the difference. "This is a lovely room," she said without thinking.

"As opposed to the other rooms in my home?" Bob asked.

"Oh, I didn't mean that," Rosie said, placing her hand over her mouth.

"Please sit down," Bob said, pointing to the love seat.

Rosie perched on the edge of the seat and put the plate of cookies on the table. Stanley sat down next to her, angling himself so she was slightly shielded from Bob. "Help yourself to a cookie," he said. "I've already snatched enough hot out of the oven that I shouldn't have another."

Laughing, he reached for one. He bit into it and his smile increased. "Oh, these are very good cookies," he said. "You know, Jeannine used to make cookies for me."

"Jeannine?" Stanley asked.

"Oh, Jeannine was the woman who disappeared," he said. "She used to be my next door neighbor."

"Oh, what ever happened to her?" Rosie asked.

Bob shrugged. "Well, the police never figured it out," he said, shaking his head. "They never asked me. I would have told them the truth."

Rosie moved closer to Stanley. "The truth?" she asked.

Bob reached out and Stanley and Rosie leaned back. Then Bob picked up another cookie.

"I can be honest with you," he said. "Can't I?"

Stanley shook his head. "Well, we're your neighbors," he said. "If you can't be honest with your neighbors, who can you be honest with?"

Nodding, Bob met Stanley's eyes. "Yes. Yes, you're right," he agreed. "Of course, if you tell anyone, they're never going to believe you anyway."

"What will no one believe?" Rosie asked.

Bob glanced around the room and then leaned forward. This time Rosie and Stanley leaned toward him. "Aliens," he said.

"Aliens?" both Rosie and Stanley repeated.

Bob slowly nodded his head and raised his eyebrows in silent agreement. "They're here, among us," he said.

"Why would they be interested in your next door neighbor?" Stanley asked.

"Because she was abducted by them and they impregnated her," he said.

"They impregnated her?" Rosie said. "She was going to have an alien baby?"

He nodded. "And you know what would happen once an alien race begins to be born?"

Rosie shook her head. "No. What?"

"They take over the world," he said. "They multiply and take us all over."

Stanley cleared his throat. "Are aliens the reason you have all that stuff in your house?"

Smiling widely, Bob turned his attention to Stanley. "Have you studied alien beings before, then?" he asked. "They don't like clutter. The clutter and garbage in my house confuses their devices, so they can't find me."

"But this room," Rosie said. "I don't understand…"

Bob looked at them and then lifted his eyes to the ceiling. "Aluminum foil."

They looked up and, sure enough, the ceiling was coated with aluminum foil.

"Does that work?" Stanley asked.

Bob shrugged. "It has so far."

"But, getting back to your neighbor," Rosie said. "How did you know about her?"

"Oh, I guessed it right away," he said. "And then, I decided I had to do something about it."

Rosie looked at Stanley. "What did you do?" she asked.

"It's better if I show you," he said. "I have it down in the basement."

Chapter Twenty-five

Mike sat in the corner of the sleeping quarters in the firehouse waiting for the change of shift. Bradley's announcement of who the John Doe had been sent a frisson of dread down his spine. Just like the other people on the force, he thought Paul Taylor was a real creep and secretly hoped the guys in prison would take care of the child killer. But to find Taylor's body in a fire that looked to be set by a professional. He was really hoping it was just coincidence, but he had to find out.

He heard footsteps coming up the stairs, the new shift was getting ready to put their gear into their lockers and catch some sleep before an alarm woke them up.

Mike looked at the professionals he'd considered friends for the past ten years of his life. Could any of them have been a murderer? Could any of them have decided to take the law into their own hands?

Most of them had dedicated their lives to the Fire Department. A couple of them were hot heads. But, they would risk their lives to save anyone else, didn't matter what their color was, what church they went to or what neighborhood they lived in. They risked it all every day.

Johnny Corbonni, who considered himself an Italian stud, was laughing as he walked over to his locker. "So, the Chief tells me he thinks Mike is haunting the firehouse," Johnny laughed. "He says his cup went flying across the room, like a missile."

"Hey, if Mike was gonna haunt someplace, it'd be the women's locker room at the Y," Pat Brennan laughed.

Mike always thought Pat looked like a matchstick, tall and skinny with a bright flame of red hair on the top of his head. But those who thought because he was thin, he was weak, were soon proved wrong.

Mike slipped past the two firemen and made his way downstairs. Maybe Chief Jack Williamson could give him some insight into the death of Paul Taylor.

He entered Jack's office and saw him standing in his private bathroom, next to the sink. He was opening up a bottle of pills and swallowing a couple of them. Mike hoped he hadn't given Jack a headache or anything. Course, considering how he'd been moving, it was probably arthritis medicine.

Mike sat down in one of the chairs in the room and looked around the room. There were family pictures, but none of them had Jack in them. He remembered some of the late evening chats where Jack had given a few of them advice about relationships.

"Boys, the job ain't worth it," he had said. "You gotta have a life. You gotta be a dad, a husband and a lover."

"So, does that mean we gotta get three different women, Chief?" Johnny had teased.

Jack smiled, but it was short-lived. "You know, I had three different women," he said. "Three wives. I tried marriage three times, and each time I was the one who let everyone down. I got kids who grew up without ever getting to know their dad."

"Hey, you had a job to do," Mike had said. "You were saving peoples' lives. You know, maybe it was the women you chose."

Jack shook his head sadly. "No, Mike. I'd like to be able to say that," he said. "But I escaped to the firehouse when life got tough. Fire and danger I could deal with. At the firehouse, I was a hero. I was a good guy. At home, I was just a guy who was supposed to deal with everyday problems. I was supposed to remember to take out the garbage, call the bank, pick up the kids at school and mow the lawn."

He ran his hand over his face. "It's a lot easier being the hero," he said. "But, in the long run, the guy who stays home and plays with his kids and loves his wife, he's the hero."

Jack had walked away from their group and closed his office door behind him.

"Damn," Pat said. "Just damn."

"Yeah," Johnny added. "I ain't ever getting married. I'm just gonna play around."

"What, you don't want no kids with the famous Corbonni schnozzola?" Pat asked.

"Hey, there ain't nothing wrong with my nose," Johnny replied, touching the side of his nose. "It's dignified."

"Yeah, so's a giant Sequoia, but I don't want one of those sticking out of the middle of my face," Pat said.

Mike hadn't participated in the argument that day, he remembered as he glanced around the walls of the office. And Jack never said anything about his family after that. He did remember hearing that one of Jack's kids got married and he hadn't been invited to the wedding. But Jack hadn't mentioned it; he just scheduled a practice drill that day and they burned down a derelict factory on the edge of town.

Just then, as Jack walked out the bathroom, the phone rang. He picked it up on the second ring and sat behind his desk.

"Chief Williamson."

Mike watched him pull a piece of paper across the table and write on it. "Paul Taylor, you say," he said into the phone. "Yeah, I remember the guy. Can't say I feel bad about this."

He wrote down a few things on the paper. "Yeah, I got it," he said. "Keep this quiet until you can get some investigators down here to question them. I got no problem with that. My people would not commit murder and they wouldn't start a fire."

He listened for a moment longer. "Yeah, I can call them in," he said. "But we had a three-alarm last night and my alternate shift is probably sound asleep. I'd really prefer you have those investigators here toward the end of the shift. That way no one talks and my people get their sleep. That work for you?"

He paused again. "No, no questions," he said. "Wait. Yeah, I do have one. Yesterday, when you were in here, was Mike with you?"

He listened and shook his head. "Damn," he said. "Guess I owe Miss O'Reilly an apology."

Mike grinned. "Good for you, Bradley," he said.

Jack hung up the phone, cradled his head in his hands and just sat there for a few minutes. Then he picked up the phone and dialed. "This is Chief Williamson," he said. "I gotta cancel my appointment for this afternoon. Yeah, something came up here at the station and I can't get away."

He listened for a moment. "Yeah, I'll call back and make another appointment," he said. "Thanks."

He had barely hung up the phone when the fire alarm sounded throughout the building. Jack jumped up and ran out of the room. "All right boys and girls, let's go put out a fire," he called to the crew slipping their gear on.

Mike waited until the fire trucks had left the building and then he faded away.

179

Chapter Twenty-six

Mary dialed the number and waited for someone to answer. "Hello, this is Mary, um, MacDougal," she said. "Bradley Alden gave me your name. We're renting from him for a little while until we find our own place and he thought you might be able to help us."

Mary smiled at Ian and nodded. "Oh, yes. Well, my husband is a professor and we're actually fairly newly married," she said. "He's been in Scotland and now we're settling here in the States."

Ian walked over next to her. "Ach, me darling, have you bin able to call up the real estate agent?" he asked loudly with a grin. "I've a strong need to have us in our own wee castle and start filling it with our own wee bairns."

Mary rolled her eyes at him and tried not to laugh.

"Yes, he actually is from Scotland," she said in the phone. "Yes, those Scots can be very impatient."

"Really, darling, I've a mind to see some houses today," he said. "Can we go down to meet her now?"

"I'm so sorry," Mary said. "Is there any chance we could come by this morning and look at some listings with you?"

Mary frowned and shook her head.

"Oh, darling, I forgot to tell you," Ian said. "The fellow at the college had a friend who's a real estate agent too. He said to give him a ring if this one's too busy."

Mary grinned. "Actually, if today doesn't work out, that's fine. No, don't worry, we have some other options."

"Oh, you can see us this morning?" she said. "Well, that's just great. Bradley told us how wonderful you were and I really would feel much more comfortable putting ourselves in your capable hands."

Mary hung up the phone and turned to Ian. "Your accent seemed suddenly more pronounced," she said.

"Aye, I was trying to be more intimidating," he said. "Do you think it worked?"

She grinned. "Well, we can go over there right now. So, yes, it worked."

"Before we go," he said, and then paused. "I feel like such a lass asking you this."

"What?"

Ian slipped off the oversized zip-up sweatshirt he'd been wearing. Mary's eyes widened as she inspected his long-sleeve black spandex turtleneck that clung tightly to his skin and emphasized every one of his ripped abs.

"Oh, my," Mary said, feeling suddenly warm. "That's a very nice shirt."

181

"Jeannine told me to wear something to emphasize my assets," he said.

"So, you don't have any spandex leggings to go with the shirt?" she asked, raising an eyebrow.

Ian blushed. "I'll not be made fun of," he said defensively, picking up the sweatshirt. "I can just as easily put this back on."

"I'm sorry," she said. "I was just teasing you. You look very good. Actually, you look sinfully good. And if Mercedes is as man hungry as Jeannine suggests, she won't be able to think straight once she gets a look at you."

"You won't be telling anyone about this?" he asked.

She shook her head. "Oh, no, Ian. Your secret is safe with me."

A few minutes later, Mary and Ian were standing in front of Mercedes's home. Mary was carrying a plate of cookies and Ian was right behind her, his arms wrapped tightly around her waist.

"What are you doing?" she asked.

"I'm being an impatient Scot," he whispered into her ear. "Besides, I'm freezing to death. How do you live in these temperatures?"

She laughed. "We're tough and we have thick blood," she said, turning her face up to his.

The door started to open and Ian slid one hand up, cupped Mary's face and placed a kiss on her lips. "Darling, we could quickly slip home and warm each other up," he said.

Mary grinned at him, comforted by the fact that although he was a very good kisser, she didn't feel any of the emotion she did when Bradley kissed her. "Sweetheart, I believe someone's answered the door."

Ian looked up and smiled at Mercedes. "Ah, well then, you can't blame a man for trying, now, can you?" he asked with a wink.

"No," she responded. "And if I were your wife, I wouldn't have cared who was opening the door."

"Aye, but if I had my way, she'd never get out of bed at all," he said with a shrug. "So, it's a good thing one of has a bit of restraint."

"Oh," Mercedes responded, her face turning red. "I suppose so."

Mary stepped forward and extended her hand. "Hello, I'm Mary," she said. "Thank you for letting us come by."

She gently nudged Ian with her elbow.

"Oh, aye, I'm Ian," he said, shaking her hand. "We do appreciate your time."

"Well, why don't we all come inside?" Mercedes said.

The house looked like something out of an Architectural Design magazine with polished wood, smoky glass and modern furnishings. "Why don't we go into the kitchen?" Mercedes suggested. "I'd like you to meet my husband, Harvey."

183

"That would be lovely," Mary said. "We brought some cookies to apologize for our last minute request to see you."

"Oh, it's no…" Mercedes started to say, and then Ian slipped out of his coat.

She swallowed and her eyes focused on his chest. "No problem at all," she said mechanically.

Ian smiled at her. "Is there a place for my coat?" he asked. "Or should I just slip it back on?"

"Oh, no!" she said, snatching it from him. "No need to put your coat back on. I'll just hang it up for you."

Jeannine appeared next to Mary and chuckled. "What did I tell you? She's a pushover for a pretty face."

"I didn't notice her staring at his face," Mary whispered.

Ian glared at Mary.

"So, Mercedes," Mary said, hefting the plate. "The kitchen?"

"Oh, sweetheart, let me take those," Ian said, stepping forward and relieving Mary of the plate. "You shouldn't be carrying anything in your condition."

"Her condition?" Mercedes asked.

"Well, we'll be looking for a house with a nursery," Mary said.

Ian slipped his arm around Mary, pulled her close and laid a kiss on her forehead. "Aye, she's making me the happiest of men," he said.

184

Mercedes sighed. "Well, come this way and meet…" her voice went flat, "Harvey, my husband."

They walked down a long hallway and into a rustic-looking kitchen with a stone floor, a commercial oven, a large double stainless steel refrigerator, granite counter tops and smoked glass cabinets.

"Wow, this kitchen is stunning," Mary said. "Do you do a lot of cooking?"

Harvey snorted. "The only thing Mercedes can cook up is the phone number to the take-out places in town."

"Aye, so you're the chef, then," Ian said.

"No, the kitchen's just for show," he said. "But you have to admit, it looks impressive."

Ian smiled. "It does."

"Harvey, this is Mary and Ian MacDougal," Mercedes said. "They're living in the Alden place for a while until they find their own home."

"So, you're neighbors," Harvey said, shaking their hands. "Welcome to the neighborhood."

Ian placed the plate on the table and helped Mary onto a stool next to the island. "We brought cookies," he said. "Mary's grandparents are staying with us for a bit and her grandmother is a genius in the kitchen. She's made far too many for us."

He patted his tight stomach, "I'm afraid I'm putting on weight."

"Not that you'd notice," Mercedes said. "So, Mary, your grandmother made the cookies. Does that mean you don't cook either?"

"Well, I dabble in the kitchen," she said.

"Ach, don't let her modesty fool you," he said. "She's brilliant in the kitchen."

He lifted her hand and placed a kiss on the palm. "She's brilliant in every room of the house."

"Laying it on a bit thick, aren't we, Ian?" Jeannine said.

Ian winked at her.

"So, what's the housing market like here?" he asked Mercedes. "I'd like to set up some appointments for next week, if possible."

"Oh, yes, that would be fine," she replied. "We have a lot of suitable houses. I just have to know your price range. I'm assuming a first-year professor."

Ian laughed. "Well, aye, it's my first year here," he said. "But I'm on loan from the University of Edinburgh. And if I were back home, we'd be living on my estate near Perth. It's a drafty pile of rocks, but it's home."

Mary chuckled. "What he meant to say is his pile of rocks sits on about 190 acres of land and is commonly known as a castle with stables, a dower house, a chapel and about four other buildings. But really, we don't need anything nearly as fancy here in the States."

"Oh, I see," Mercedes said. "So, you will be looking for an executive home."

"Aye," Ian said. "And my first concern is security. I'm not taking any chances with Mary."

"Oh, you don't have to worry about security in this area," Mercedes insisted. "Why, we have one of the lowest crime rates in the state."

"And yet Bradley's wife was taken from his home only eight years ago," Ian said. "That doesn't worry you?"

"He's got a point there, Dee," Harvey said to his wife. "You just never know about some things."

"She didn't get taken," Mercedes said. "She ran away. Everyone knew she was having an affair. Only poor Bradley was unaware."

"Oh, that's odd," Mary said. "I hadn't heard the mystery had been solved."

Mercedes shrugged. "Well, if you don't want to be found it's very easy to disappear in the United States."

"I've met Bradley," Ian said. "Doesn't seem like the kind of fellow a woman would run away from."

"Well," Mercedes purred. "Some women can't handle that much man."

"Rip her hair out for me, Mary," Jeannine said, "all the way to her gray roots."

"Speaking of Bradley," Mary said, deciding it was wise to change the subject. "He told us you had won some awards in real estate. Ian didn't even realize there were such things."

"Well, it's not like it's an Olympic sport," he said. "Do they really give awards for selling houses?"

187

Mercedes stiffened. "Well, not just for selling houses," she said, "but for selling millions of dollars' worth of houses."

"Aye, and that's a fair number of houses here in the States, is it?" he asked.

"Yes, they are prestigious awards," she replied.

"And do they look like wee mansions?" Ian asked. "The awards I mean."

"I could show them to you, if you'd like," she said. "They're in my office."

He turned to Mary. "Do you mind, darling? We won't be but a moment."

She smiled. "No, I'll be fine," she said. "And Harvey and I can get better acquainted."

He placed a kiss on her cheek. "Think of me."

"Good grief," Jeannine said. "Really, Ian, this is too much."

Ian chuckled and followed Mercedes out of the room.

"Can I get you something to drink?" Harvey offered.

"Some water would be perfect," Mary replied.

Harvey walked across the room to get a glass from the cabinet and Mary turned to Jeannine. "Do you recognize any of the baskets?" she whispered, motioning to a shelf displaying a number of woven baskets.

Jeannine glided over to the shelf and took her time looking at the various baskets. In the meantime, Harvey came back with a glass of ice water. "Thank you," Mary said, taking a sip. "Did you know Jeannine?"

Harvey nodded. "Yeah, she was a sweetheart," he said. "Bradley was a lucky guy. If I had a woman like that in my life, I'd never let her go."

Mary smiled. "Yes, but you have a lovely wife too," she said. "Mercedes seems so…energetic."

Harvey shrugged. "Well, Mercedes is the kind of woman who is not content with just one man," he said. "And I guess I've accepted that."

Mary saw the hurt on his face and instinctively placed her hand on his for comfort. "I'm sorry," she said. "That must be difficult sometimes."

He looked down at her hand covering his and then looked up in her eyes. "Well, she lets me have my little hobbies too," he said, placing his other hand on top of hers. "Some women wouldn't put up with my, shall I say, unusual habits. I would be happy to show them to you someday. I keep them in the basement."

Chapter Twenty-seven

Ian and Mary arrived back at the house at the same time Rosie and Stanley were making their way back up the driveway. No one said a word; they all just hurried inside and waited to speak until the door was firmly closed behind them.

"We know who did it," they all said simultaneously.

"No, we know who did it," they argued in chorus.

"No! We know who did it," they emphatically stated.

"Okay, stop!" Mary yelled. "This is not getting us anywhere."

"You're right," Stanley said. "'Specially since half of this room is wrong."

"Oh, I thought we were right, Stanley," Rosie said.

Stanley rolled his eyes. "No, Rosie, we are the ones who are right. They are wrong."

Rosie sighed with relief. "Well, good, because I really would hate to have put up with that horrid place only to realize we were wrong."

"There ain't no way on earth we're wrong," Stanley said.

"Well, I don't know what your experience was like," Ian said, taking his coat off and hanging it up. "But I was very nearly mauled by an oversexed she-cat, just so Mary could have a few minutes alone with Harvey and find out that he did it."

"Maybe iffen you didn't wear shirts that showed off your man boobies the women wouldn't act so crazy," Stanley said, then he grabbed the lapels of his brushed cotton flannel shirt. "You should wear respectable shirts like mine."

"I don't know," Rosie said, with a shy smile at Ian. "I really like his shirt."

"Why don't we all just sit down?" Mary suggested. "And then we can talk about our experiences."

They settled in the living room, Rosie and Stanley sharing the love seat, Mary in the recliner and Ian on the couch in front of the computer.

"Do you think we ought to have Sean and Bradley share in the conversation?" Ian asked. "They might give us a different perspective."

"Yeah, they can tell you that Rosie and I found the murderer," Stanley said.

Ian placed a call through video conferencing to both Sean and Bradley, but only Sean answered.

"Hey, Ian, how's it going?" he asked. "Nice shirt, by the way. Your man boobies are looking fairly fit."

"Oh, and everyone's a funny man today," Ian said. "You've obviously been watching our conversation through the camera feeds…"

"What makes you say that?" Sean asked.

"Funny, Sean. Funny," Ian said. "Now try to mature a little in the next few moments because we need you to listen to our various experiences and tell us what you think."

"Okay, let's hear what happened."

Stanley and Rosie took turns explaining what happened to them at Bob's house.

"What did you do when he invited you down to the basement?" Mary asked.

"Well, you know I would have gone down there iffen Rosie wasn't there, needing my protection," Stanley said.

"Oh, Stanley," Rosie said, placing her hand on his leg. "That would have been so dangerous. I'm so glad you didn't do it."

He smiled at her and placed his hand over hers. "Don't worry, girlie, I ain't about to take any unnecessary risks. I'm finally realizing I got a whole lot to live for."

Rosie blushed. "Oh, Stanley."

Realizing the others were waiting for him, he cleared his throat loudly and continued. "As I was saying, Bob wanted us to go down to the basement with him to show us how he could prove Jeannine had been impregnated by aliens," Stanley said. "I told him that Rosie and I would really like to come, but wouldn't it better if we wore some kind of protective gear so our thoughts wouldn't be susceptible to surveillance."

"Wasn't that brilliant of him?" Rosie asked.

"And luckily for us, he was out of aluminum foil," Stanley said. "So, I think all we need to do is break into his house and check out the basement."

"Well, done, Stanley and Rosie," Sean said. "I agree with you this fellow could potentially be the kidnapper. Usually in cases like this, when the perpetrator feels the victim could actually put him at risk, he tends to kill the victim immediately and not transport him to his own home. However, that's not the case 100 percent of the time, so Bob sounds like a person of interest."

"Yes, he does sound like he's an excellent candidate," Ian said. "And I can assure you that Mary and I did not have to put up with the kind of environment you were in. Although at least one of our hosts was not as gracious as yours."

Ian and Mary related the events that occurred at Mercedes and Harvey's house.

"So, why didn't you go down to the basement with him?" Rosie asked.

"Well, Ian came rushing back into the room," Mary said, trying to hide her smile. "His shirt was slightly askew and he looked like he'd been wrestling."

"It's not funny," he said. "The woman is a menace, she thinks she's irresistible and means to prove it."

"Well, actually, having a woman like that paired with a partner who is little off-kilter could present another good scenario," Sean said. "If

Mercedes saw Jeannine as competition, she could have encouraged Harvey's fantasies."

"So, what do you suggest we do next?" Mary asked.

"Well, I'll run the records on these suspects," Sean said. "Anyone else on your list you want me to check?"

"No," Mary said. "It seems like Gary is simply a harmless, lonely man. I think he fell off the suspect list once we met the other people on the list."

"It's just as easy for me to check out four as it is three," Sean said.

Mary shrugged. "Okay, sure, check out Gary Copper. He's a dentist out here."

"So, what do we do while Sean runs their records?" Stanley asked. "I don't want to just do nothing when we are this close."

Rosie smiled and clapped her hands. "Oh, I know," she said. "We should have a dinner party, like they do in the Agatha Christie mysteries. Bring everyone together and see how they react with each other. Maybe we can drop some kind of bombshell and see how they react."

Mary considered Rosie's idea for a moment.

"You know, that's not a bad idea," she said. "Instead of dinner, we could do a brunch, then it's done in the light of day. And we could have it on Saturday, so no one would be at work. What do you think, Sean?"

"As long as you are all careful, especially with food preparation," he said. "We know Jeannine was drugged and we don't want that happening to you."

"There's no way someone would be able to drug us, Sean," Mary said. "Don't worry."

Chapter Twenty-eight

"It's really no big deal," Mary insisted, standing in the kitchen with Rosie. "I stop by Bob's and just invite him to the brunch. I don't go inside; I just stand in the doorway. Then, I'll go over to Gary's office with a plate of cookies and invite him too. All daytime. All safe. All with people around."

"I really think someone should go with you," Rosie said.

"You and Stanley have to go grocery shopping and Ian has to calibrate the bugs we placed today," Mary said. "And, really, this is no big deal. Remember, I've been trained."

"Ach, no, I can't stand it," Ian's cry came from the other room.

They hurried in to find Ian shaking his head and Stanley chuckling.

"What's wrong?" Mary asked.

Stanley leaned over and turned up the volume on Ian's computer and the room was filled with an off-key and very sharp version of a Scottish love song:

O ye'll tak the high road and I'll tak the low road,
An' I'll be in Scotland afore ye;
But me and my true love will never meet again
On the bonnie, bonnie banks o' Loch Lomond.

"Many a buried Scot are turning in their graves on the hearing of this," Ian said.

"Well, obviously you and your man boobies made quite an impression," Mary teased, sitting down next to Ian on the couch.

"One more crack about me man boobies and I'll suggest we serve haggis for the brunch," he whispered to Mary.

She turned and smiled at him. "It's a good thing I'm pregnant and can't eat any organ meat for fear of harming the baby," she countered.

"Ah, Mary O'Reilly, you're a fair wicked minx," he said. "And you have me on that one. Perhaps I'll let Bradley know I had the pleasure of tasting your lips a number of times today."

"And I'll tell him truthfully that it was like kissing my brother," she said with a grin. "No harm intended."

"None taken," he said. "And, aye, I felt the same way. You're a bonnie lass, but you're not my Gillian and there's the rub."

She leaned over and placed a kiss on his cheek. "You're a good sport, Ian MacDougal. Now, you just need to call Mercedes and invite them over for Saturday brunch."

"Oh, you've a mean streak a mile wide," he said.

"Think of it this way," she said, as she rose from the couch. "If she's on the phone with you, she can't sing."

Mary grabbed her coat, the final plate of cookies and her purse. "I have my cell phone," she said. "So if you need to contact me, just call. I shouldn't be very long at all."

She dropped her purse and the plate off in the car before she trudged across the snow to Bob's house. Knocking on the door, she thought about the experience Rosie and Stanley had undergone and a shudder went through her body. There was no way she would step foot inside this house if she didn't have to.

The door opened slightly and Mary recognized the man from Jeannine's memories. "Hello," she said with a bright smile. "I'm Mary, Mary MacDougal, from next door. I believe you met my grandparents today."

The door opened wider. "Yes, I did," he said. "Would you like to come in?"

"I'm sorry," Mary said, with what she hoped sounded like real regret. "I'm just on my way out to run some errands. But, I wanted to stop here and invite you over to our house on Saturday at eleven for a brunch."

His smile was genuine. "Really? A brunch?" he said. "I haven't been out of the house in so long. I would love to come. Can I bring something?"

"No. I mean, no thank you," Mary said, tempering her first response and placing her hand on his arm. "Grandma loves to cook and she is in heaven planning the menu. So, just bring yourself and your appetite."

"Thank you, I will," Bob said.

Just then Ian ran out of the house and jogged over to Bob's. "I worried when I saw you on the stairs," he said. "I didn't want you slipping and falling."

"Bob, this is my husband, Ian," she said. "And he's a little overprotective."

"Well, she is expecting our first baby," he explained. "And I can't help but feel I want to wrap her up in cotton and store her away some place safe."

Bob nodded and met Ian's eyes. "Yes, I know just how you feel."

Chapter Twenty-nine

Bradley scanned through the electronic file he received on Paul Taylor. There was no doubt about it, the guy was a creep. The only reason he'd been released early was because he wasn't considered a threat to society in general. "Yeah, only to his wife and three kids," Bradley muttered.

He brought up the photos again. A smiling young mother sat behind her three beautiful children, two boys and a little girl. Bradley studied the little girl; she looked like she was about eight years old. Would his daughter look anything like her?

"She was still pretty, even in death," Mike said over Bradley's shoulder.

Bradley jumped and then turned to Mike. "Do you have to do that?"

Mike shook his head. "No, but it really makes things much more fun."

"Where did you go the other night?" Bradley asked.

Mike floated across the room and settled on the couch. "Come on, Chief, we both know where I went."

Bradley nodded. "So, did you find anything out at the fire station? Anything that you would be willing to share with me?"

Mike grinned. "Yeah, you're not stupid," he said. "Actually, no, I was surprised. I figured I'd walk in on this big conspiracy. But the biggest news of the day is that I'm haunting the station. Go figure."

"So, you thought one of the firemen might be behind this too?" he asked.

Mike shrugged. "The guy was a murderer and we got to go in and pick up the remains of what he did. Firefighting is about saving lives. We all risked our lives that night because this bastard decides he wants to get rid of his responsibilities and we all had to try and live with the fact there was nothing we could do. That's not easy for firefighters."

Mike floated back over to Bradley and gazed at the picture on the screen. "I found her," he said. "She was dressed in a pink flannel nightgown and she had a pink ribbon in her hair. Her room was filled with stuffed animals and dolls. I was so relieved I had gotten to her before the fire. I was so grateful she was going to live to go to her high school prom. Then I picked her up in my arms and she was limp. I pulled my mask off, so I could check for her breathing, and that's when I saw the purple marks on her neck and noticed that her lips were blue. I can't explain to you the kind of rage I felt at that moment. If that guy had been close, I don't know what I would have done."

"You would have done what you were supposed to do," Bradley said. "Training and civility always wins."

Mike shook his head. "Not always. Not always."

Bradley clicked on the next photo, the one of the family, and Mike inhaled sharply.

"What?" Bradley asked.

He stepped back and shook his head again. "Never saw the family photo before," he said. "Never saw them all together like that. They were a beautiful family."

Bradley nodded. "Yeah, they were. So, what do you think the next step should be?"

Closing his eyes, Mike took a moment and then met Bradley's eyes squarely. "I might have a lead," he said. "But I need to follow it up on my own."

"You want me to trust you to follow up on this case, even though it might include the people you consider family?" Bradley asked.

Mike nodded. "Yes, that's what I'm asking."

"Well, I know you're a good and honest man," he said. "Just let me know if you need my help."

"Thank you," Mike said. "That means a lot to me. I'll contact you when I can."

The fire station was dark when Mike faded into the main garage. Emergency lights cast an eerie glow on the large trucks and emergency equipment. Mike felt a little hesitant moving forward.

"Oh, wait,' he said. "I'm the ghost in the room. I'm not supposed to get freaked out."

He walked past the kitchen and the stairs to the sleeping quarters and made his way to the Chief's office. Once through the door, he looked around the

202

room, searching and finding the item he had come for. On the second shelf, behind the Chief's desk was a framed photo of the Chief's daughter and his three grandchildren. The same photo he had seen on Bradley's computer just a few minutes ago.

Chapter Thirty

The drive to Gary's office in downtown Sycamore took about fifteen minutes. The sun was already beginning to set by the time Mary rushed through the parking lot and into the Waiting Room. An older gray-haired woman sat at the reception desk and greeted Mary as she came through the door.

"Hello," she said. "I'm sorry, but we are closing for the day. Could I help you make another appointment?"

Mary came forward, smiling. "Oh, I'm sorry to be a bother. Actually, I'm not a patient, I'm one of Gary's neighbors and I wanted to drop by a plate of cookies. My name is Mary MacDougal."

"Well, isn't that the sweetest thing," the receptionist said. "I'm sure he'll be delighted. Let me buzz him, he's just in his office finishing up his paperwork."

She pressed the intercom button. "Dr. Copper, there's a nice lady here to see you. She even brought you cookies. Should I send her back to you or do you want to come up?"

"I'll be up in a minute, Shirley," the slightly mechanized voice responded.

Mary felt an uneasy feeling wash over her. Her heart rate accelerated slightly and she felt as if she were trapped in the room. She took a couple deep breaths and tried to calm down. She'd never felt claustrophobic before.

"The doctor will be up here in a minute," the receptionist said. "Would you like to sit down?"

Nodding, Mary started to turn away when she lost her equilibrium. The room started to tilt and the plate of cookies she was holding fell from her hands onto the floor. She grabbed for the counter and the room continued to sway. A moment later, she found herself leaning against Gary and being guided to one of the chairs in the waiting area. "I'm so sorry," she whispered. "I don't know what came over me."

"Oh, well, those first few months of pregnancy can do crazy things to your hormones and your body," Gary said. "Do you want to just lie down here for a while and rest? Shirley is going home now, but I could take you home when I close up in thirty minutes."

She tried to clear her head. All she could think of was Bradley's response to her staying alone with one of the suspects in a murder trial, even though he was the least likely to have done it. "I think he'd kill me," she muttered.

"Excuse me?" Gary said. "I've never…"

She quickly realized what she said. "No, I meant that Ian would kill me if I didn't call him. He's very overprotective."

Gary smiled and nodded. "Well, of course he is. Do you want me to call him?"

Mary reached into her pocket and pulled out her cell phone. "No, I can do it," she said. "But thank you, Gary."

She called his number and it only took him one ring to pick up. "What's up?" he asked in a cheery voice.

"Well, it seems I've encountered some difficulty," she said.

"Mary, where are you and what's wrong?" the tenor in his voice changed immediately and his strength was reassuring.

"I'm at Gary's office," she said. "Something happened, suddenly I was very dizzy."

"Like drugged dizzy?" he asked.

"Maybe," she said. "I can't walk."

"I'll be there in ten minutes," he said.

"Ian, it takes fifteen," she said with a slight smile.

"I'll be there in ten."

She hung up the phone and slid it back in her pocket. "Ian's on his way," she said. "I truly apologize for the bother and, oh, for the cookies."

She looked beyond Gary and saw the plate on the floor and most of the cookies scattered around it.

Gary chuckled. "Oh, don't worry about those," he said. "It looks like quite a few are still fine and losing some will save me from overeating."

Mary smiled. "Thank you, while I'm having a moment of coherence I need to invite you to the brunch we are having Saturday morning. It will be at eleven and my grandmother is already planning the menu."

"That's sounds very nice," he said. "May I bring something along?"

Mary smiled, but shook her head. "Normally I would say yes, but this time it's my grandmother's party, so I dare not."

"Well, I would be delighted to accept your invitation."

Standing, he pulled a chair across the room so Mary could put her feet up. "Are you comfortable? Do you need a blanket or some water?" he asked.

Shaking her head, she realized she was feeling a little bit better. "No, thank you. But you know, I think I'm feeling a bit better."

"Well, you just sit there until Ian arrives. Let's not take any chances."

True to his word, ten minutes after she'd hung up with him Ian burst through the door. He immediately saw Mary and rushed to her side. "How are you feeling?" he asked, cradling her face in his hand.

"A little silly," she replied.

"Ah, well then, you must be doing better. Silly is two steps up from dizzy."

Ian turned to Gary. "I owe you my thanks for taking care of her," he said, and shook Gary's hand.

"No problem, she was a model patient," he replied. "I'd be happy to take care of her anytime."

Ian turned back to Mary. "Shall we go home now?"

She nodded, started to rise and squealed when Ian scooped her up in his arms. "Ian, I can walk," she said. "I'm barely dizzy at all."

He hoisted her higher in his arms and she threw her arms around his neck to hold on. "Aye, now that's better, me darling," he said. "No more lip from you until we get you back home."

"But Ian," she said, "I can walk."

"I have to use the man boobies for something, darling, else they're just for show," he whispered.

She giggled.

"That's a girl," he said. "Now put your head on my shoulder and snuggle in tight. I'll get you to the car safely."

She did as he requested and had to admit that she did feel a wave of well-being when she was held in his arms. "This is so not me," she whispered, as Ian carried her through the parking lot. "I kick butt, I don't faint."

He chuckled into her hair. "Well, if you tried kicking just now you'd be sitting on your butt, I'd say."

He put her on her feet outside the car and opened the door for her. She climbed into her seat and buckled herself in. Ian went around and got in the car and started it up. Then he turned to her, his face suddenly serious. "So, tell me. What happened in there?"

Mary shook her head. "I seriously have no idea," she said. "One moment I'm standing at the counter, asking for Gary, the next moment the world has gone all tilt-a-whirl."

"Did you feel faint when you walked up the stairs?"

"No, I felt fine," she said. "Honestly, there was nothing."

"And how are you feeling now?"

She took a deep breath and did a self-assessment. "A little shaky," she said. "But for the most part, I feel fine. I can tell you for a few moments in there, I didn't feel like myself at all."

Ian paused. "Well, then, maybe you weren't."

"Maybe I wasn't what?"

"Maybe you weren't yourself," he said. "You and Jeannine have bonded, so to speak. You not only allowed her to share your body, but you shared her memories. Those memories are now your memories too. Something that happened today might have triggered a delayed response in you and your body reacted."

Mary nodded. "Well, considering that I've met with all of the potential suspects on our short list that makes sense. So, it was just a one-time thing."

"Well, that's what I'm hoping," Ian said. "Could be, because you have her memories, that this might be a recurring issue for you."

"Well, crap," she said.

"Aye, crap indeed."

Chapter Thirty-one

Mike opened his eyes and looked around the room. This was certainly the Christopher Columbus method of haunting; materialize in a place and then find out where it is. The house was tiny and everything seemed worn. It had the feel of a bachelor pad, no knickknacks or feminine touches to make it feel like home.

He moved to the kitchen. The countertop was filled with an assortment of cereals, snack foods and dirty dishes. The kitchen table was stacked with newspapers. The older model white refrigerator was a little dingy, but it was free of magnets, pictures and take-out menus, except for two newspaper articles that were taped to the door with duct tape. The first one was about the murder of the Taylor family. The paper was slightly yellow and there were a few small stains on the edges, but the photo was the same as Mike had seen in the Chief's office and on Bradley's computer. The other article was a small piece about the release of Paul Taylor on good behavior.

Mike took a deep breath and nodded. "Yeah, it didn't take a genius to figure this one out."

He moved through the kitchen and stopped by the bathroom. A nightlight had been left on and it shone on the counter that was clear except for a water glass and several containers of prescription pills.

Mike lifted the first, expecting something for arthritis. The bottle read, "Oxycontin." He remembered that was powerful stuff. Jack's arthritis must be pretty painful for him to be on that kind of stuff.

He picked up the second bottle. It was labeled "Nexavar." What the hell was Nexavar for?

"That you, Mike?"

Mike dropped the bottle with a clatter and turned. Jack was standing in the hallway, watching him.

"Can you see me?" Mike asked.

Jack continued to peer around. "Mike, is that you?" he repeated.

Mike looked around and saw the wall-sized mirror was in need of a good cleaning, which was perfect for his purposes. "YES CHIEF IT'S ME, MIKE," he wrote on the mirror.

Jack came over and flicked on the bathroom light. The printing could be clearly seen. "Well, I'll be damned," he said. "How ya doing, kid?"

Mike picked up the bottle of Nexavar and held it in front of Jack's face.

"Oh, that," he shrugged. "I always thought I'd die in a fire. You know, blaze of glory. But instead it looks like cancer is going to get me. I got colon cancer, Mike. I don't have much more time. The drugs don't fix it; they just ease some of the pain."

"DAMN," Mike scribbled quickly on the mirror.

Jack chuckled. "Yeah, I feel the same way. But, hell, at least I wasn't poisoned by some kookie woman."

Mike laughed. "GOOD ONE," he wrote.

Mike moved past Jack and back into the kitchen. He picked up the article and brought it with him to the bathroom. "YOUR DAUGHTER?"

"Yeah, I figured that's why you were here," he said. "You kinda like that ghost of Christmas past? Come to show me my evil ways?"

"NO JUST TRYING TO UNDERSTAND," he wrote. "YOU TAUGHT ME TO SAVE LIVES."

"I was a bad father," he said. "No I was a damn bad father. I missed pretty much everything from ball games to graduations. There was always a fire, always a drill, always something. My kids grew up and they didn't even know me."

He moved past Mike and sat on the closed toilet seat. "Sorry, can't stand up too long these days," he explained. "So, anyway, I kind of just lived my life and let them live theirs. But as I started to get older, I realized that work don't give you the same kind of memories that families do."

He cradled his head in his hands and sat there for a few minutes. "Mike, I decided to reach out," he said. "Decided I needed to get to know my kids and my grandkids. I needed to beg their forgiveness and try to start fresh."

He took a deep breath, coughed a few times and looked up at the mirror. "My damn hand was on the phone when we got the call for the fire," he said.

"The fire that took their lives. I never got that chance, Mike. I never got to make it better...until now."

"WHERE DID YOU GET THE PHOTO?"

Jack laughed. "Yeah, you are smarter than you look," he said. "I got it from the evidence box. I put it up there in my office the day after I killed the son-of-a-bitch. I figured someone would see it after I was gone and put two and two together. I just didn't count on that damn trough falling down and messing up my plan."

"HOW DID YOU DO IT?"

Jack laughed bitterly and reached over for the first bottle. "Did you know that it's easy to overdose on these little pills?" he asked. "And when they're crushed and mixed with a drink it works even better. Makes it seem like the person had a heart attack."

He shook the bottle in his hand. "It shouldn't be that easy to kill a man. But it was, damn easy."

"SO WHAT DO WE DO NEXT?"

Jack shook his head. "Oh, no, Mike," he said. "You gotta do what you know is right. And I won't fault you for it one bit."

Mike looked at the man before him. The man who had guided him and taught him as he worked as a fireman. The man who was like a second father to him. What the hell was he going to do?

"YOU'RE NOT GOING TO DO ANYTHING STUPID, ARE YOU?"

Jack laughed. "No, I ain't about to take the easy way out, Mike," he said. "You do what you have to do and I'll deal with it."

"YOU'RE STILL MY HERO, JACK."
Jack wiped a tear from his eye. "Thank you, Mike, that really means a lot to me."

Chapter Thirty-two

Mary nestled deeper into the pillows and cradled the laptop against her legs. She had a cup of tea and a small plate of cookies within reach and she had been ordered to get some rest. She knew it was only nine o'clock, but she hoped Bradley was already home. She clicked on the video conferencing and called his computer. A moment later Bradley's face appeared on the screen.

"Hi," she said, covering a yawn.

"Hi, yourself. What are you up too?"

"Oh, I'm laying here about to turn in and I thought I'd give you a call."

"Your life is so boring you have to go to bed at nine?" he asked.

"Yeah, I've been ordered to take some R&R," she said without thinking.

"Why?" Bradley asked. "What's wrong? What happened?"

"Nothing happened," she said firmly. "It's just been a couple of busy days, preceded by a couple of busy weeks and there was nothing going on tonight, so I'm getting extra sleep."

Bradley took an audible breath of relief. "Sorry, I tend to get a little overprotective."

"You think?" she said with a smile.

"So how's the investigation going?" he asked.

She nodded and snuggled back against the pillows. "Actually, I think it's going very well. We have a short list of suspects," she paused and yawned again. "We've visited all of them and they are all coming to a brunch on Saturday morning."

"Let me get this straight," he said. "You're going to have a group of possible murderers in your home on Saturday morning and you think that's a good thing?"

"Well, not when you put it that way," she said. "But we want to expose them to a couple of things and see if they react."

"Are you putting yourself at risk?"

Mary shook her head. "No, we have total control of the situation," she said. "Rosie is doing all of the cooking, Jeannine is going to be there to let us know if anything they say or do reminds her of something and the rest of us are just going to be friendly and ask questions. Piece of cake."

"What?"

"What do you mean, what?" she asked, her eyes beginning to close.

"What is it that you are not telling me, that you think I'm going to worry about?"

"Nothing," she said, blinking her eyes awake.

Bradley snorted. "I was watching the camera earlier this evening when you came home with Ian."

"Crap," she muttered.

"So?"

"Ian's heavy weights weren't delivered, so he takes turns carrying us around instead?" she tried.

"Mary."

"Okay, I had a thing today," she admitted.

"Really, Bradley, I'm just about asleep here."

"A thing?"

"Yeah, well, Ian thinks it could be related to Jeannine using my body when she's hypnotized."

"What the hell?"

"Oh, that's right, that's another one of those things I didn't tell you about, right? I must be more tired than I realized."

"Well, it must be exhausting to have to keep all of these secrets," he replied. "What are you thinking?"

"I'm thinking that we need to find out who did this to Jeannine and the only way we could hypnotize her is to allow her to enter my body. We talked about the risks, we took precautions and we proceeded in a scientific and controlled environment," she said, then yawned once again. "And quite frankly, I don't appreciate your attitude."

"You're right," he said.

"And another thing... Wait, what did you say?" she asked.

He sighed. "You're right," he repeated. "Trying to protect you is a gut reaction. I need to remember that you are a very capable woman."

She smiled. "Thank you," she said. "I don't mind knowing that you want to protect me. I actually like that. But I don't like feeling you are questioning my decisions."

"Can I just say that I have never questioned your intelligence or your courage?" he said. "When I do…worry…it's when you try to conquer the world on your own, without asking for help. Risk more than you need to risk."

"Yeah, I can understand that," she said, then chuckled sleepily. "You would have been proud of me this afternoon. I actually asked for help. I got dizzy for some reason and Ian drove over and rescued me. I almost didn't call, but then I thought, 'If Bradley finds out, he'll kill me.'"

"So Ian got to rescue you today?" he said.

She sighed and nestled into the blankets. "It would have been better if it had been you."

He smiled. "Good answer."

She covered a yawn and shook her head. "Sorry, I can't keep my eyes open."

"I miss you," he said.

She smiled sleepily. "I miss you too."

"Even with Ian there?" Bradley hated himself for asking, but he couldn't forget how cozy she looked being carried in Ian's arms.

"Uh-hmmmm," she murmured, her eyes slowly closing. "Although he has nice shirts."

"Nice shirts?"

She smiled widely in her half-sleep state. "Bradley, you don't have any black spandex turtlenecks do you?"

"Spandex shirts?"

"Oh, yes," she purred, snuggling into the pillows. "Tight spandex shirts."

"Mary? What the hell…?"

"Good night, Bradley," she said with a dreamy sigh. "Sweet dreams."

The screen went blank, but Bradley stared at it for a few more moments. Then he flipped over to view the cameras for the rest of the house. He searched the living room, the laundry room, the dining room and then, ah, there he was, in the kitchen. Ian was behind the refrigerator door, obviously looking for a snack. Bradley could only see the back of his shirt. It was black. Then Ian closed the door and turned to face the camera.

"Well, damn," Bradley said.

Chapter Thirty-three

Mike faded into Bradley's living room and watched him for a while. His mind was awhirl with so many things. What if this was what he was still on earth for? What if this is what was holding him here on earth?

Could he take the chance of telling Bradley the truth and then be moved on and never see Mary again? Did he want to move on? Did he really need to move on right now?

And why should Jack be punished when he only had a few months to live anyway? Why the hell didn't they give that jerk the death penalty in the first place?

He sighed. He knew what he had to do. He knew it when Bradley placed his confidence in him. He realized he knew it even before he left Jack's.

Gliding over to Bradley, Mike leaned forward and looked over his shoulder.

"Why are you looking at black spandex shirts?" he asked.

Bradley quickly closed the page. "Never mind," he said. "What do you need?"

"Well, I've got a story to tell you," Mike said. "And I want you to listen to all of it without making a decision until the end."

Bradley sat back and listened as Mike explained Jack's story.

"So, bottom line, he killed him," Bradley said.

Mike shrugged. "Yes, he did."

"Well, damn, that's not what I wanted to hear. I like Jack."

"Yeah, me too. He was kind of a second father to me."

"And I really hate the bastard he killed," Bradley admitted. "The guy deserved the death penalty."

Mike nodded. "Yeah, he did. But, that's not what the court system gave him."

"Yes, and we were both sworn to uphold the law."

"Yes, we were," Mike agreed. "And so was Jack."

"But you don't think he should be punished for this?" Bradley asked.

Shaking his head, Mike tossed his hands in defeat. "I don't know. Obviously I must think the truth needs to be out there because I came to you. But, on the other hand, I think the guy got what he deserved."

"What the hell do you want me to do about it?"

"Damned if I know," Mike said. "But I'm just the dead guy here."

"Is there any danger…?"

"Of Jack killing himself?" Mike finished. "No, he said he wasn't going to take a coward's way out."

"Well, I got to think about this one," Bradley said. "Because right now, I don't know what I want to do."

"Yeah, well let me know when you decide, okay?"

Bradley nodded. "You'll be the first one."

"Thanks."

Chapter Thirty-four

The light in the basement room was switched on once again and the lock was slid in place. But this time there were no careful steps taken to plan for the perfect night. This time the chair was dragged over to the freezer and the door was thrown open.

"I found her," he said to the frozen corpse. "I told you I would and I did. And she's perfect."

He took a deep breath and then slowly rolled his tongue over his lips. "She's going to taste so good," he said. "And she's going to feel so good. It's been such a long time."

He wiped his sweating palms against the knees of his pants. "And she touched me today," he said. "It was her way of telling me that we were meant to be together. It was her way of telling me that she wanted to be mine."

He looked at the corpse and his lips curled into a sneer. "You said no one would ever want me. You said women cringe when I touch them. You said the only way I could have a woman was if I drugged her."

He sat back in the chair and laughed, a high-pitched girlish laugh. "You're so wrong and I'm so right," he said in a sing-song voice. "You're so dead and I'm so alive."

He sat forward on the chair. "Her name is Mary and she is pregnant. Just like you were, she's pregnant. And I'm going to keep her all to myself. She'll like that. And I'll help her keep the baby safe and strong. And I love them. I'll love them both."

He reached up and took the white box from the shelf and opened it. "Guess what little girl," he said to the frozen embryo. "You're going to be a sister. You're going to be a big sister."

He put the top back on the box and placed it carefully on the shelf. Then he turned back to the corpse. "I may not be able to visit for a while," he said. "I have to get things ready for Mary. But when she's ready, I'll bring her here to meet you and then we can be a family."

He started to close the door, and then paused. "Oh, no, she can't live here," he said. "She's going to be my new bride. We need the bridal suite. We need time to be alone."

He laughed and rubbed his hands together. "We need time to get to know each other, intimately."

He closed the freezer door and hurried up the stairs, leaving the latch to the room unlocked.

Chapter Thirty-five

"So, how are we feeling this morning, Mary, me darling?" Ian asked as Mary came down the stairs.

"Fine, I'm feeling great," she said. "I had a good night's sleep and I'm ready to get going with Jeannine."

Rosie put a plate filled with bacon and eggs on the table. "Mary, dear, I've made you some breakfast. Sit down and eat while it's hot."

Mary sat down at the table, stabbed a fork into her scrambled eggs and began to lift it to her mouth when she noticed that all eyes were on her. She put the fork down and sighed. "What now?" she asked.

"I can't do it," Ian said. "I can't let you be hypnotized with Jeannine again. It's just too dangerous."

"Yep, we were all discussing it last night and we all feel that it's not the best thing for you to do," Stanley said.

"We don't want you to get hurt, dear," Rosie finished.

Mary sat back in her chair and looked around at her friends. She realized their motivation was their concern for her, but she really couldn't let that get in the way of discovering who murdered Jeannine.

"First, I want to thank you for your concern, I really appreciate it," she said. "And I know the only reason you don't want me to be hypnotized is because of what happened to me yesterday. So, what I need from all of you are your ideas on how I can get the same information without being hypnotized."

She leaned forward and placed her arms on the table. "Stanley, what do you think?"

He shrugged. "Well, maybe Jeannine could use someone else, like me," he said. "That way you could listen to what was going on rather than live it."

"Ian would that work?" Mary asked.

Ian shook his head. "No, it's not likely," he said with a sigh. "The only reason this works now is because of Mary's connection with Jeannine. It's doubtful we could recreate that same kind of bond with anyone else."

"And, I have to add," Mary said. "That because I'm actually living Jeannine's memories when she's being hypnotized I get even more information and detail than I would if I were just listening to her."

She turned to Rosie. "Rosie, what would you suggest?"

"Is there a way to get any more information from the suspects?" Rosie asked. "Pay them another visit?"

"Well, I could wait until tonight and try to break in to each of the suspects homes and check out their basements," Mary suggested. "But other than that, and the bugging Ian's already done, I don't think another visit will do us much good. Stanley, what do you think?"

"You wouldn't have to be the one to break in," Stanley said. "We could help you."

Mary held back her smile. "Stanley, I think you and Rosie might be a little rusty at breaking and entering," she said. "And I don't believe the professor has a lot of experience as a cat burglar."

Ian shook his head. "Too many years spent in a library, I suppose," he said. "But, if you want me to be there, I'd be willing."

"And you'd probably set off all the alarms in the neighborhood," Stanley grumbled.

"Oh, dear, we really aren't getting anywhere," Rosie said. "I just don't want anything to happen to you. But it seems to me that maybe having you hypnotized is the best idea."

Mary turned to Ian. "So, how about you? Do you have any suggestions to replace what we originally planned?"

"No, I don't like it," he said. "But I can see this is the safest route of all. Perhaps after this is all done I can hypnotize you and remove any of the memories you don't want to have mixed with yours."

"That would be good," Mary said. "I don't need someone else's scary situations, I have enough of my own."

She pulled her plate back in front of her. "So, are we all good now?" she asked.

They all nodded.

"Good, because I'm starving!"

An hour later, Mary was lying on the couch and Ian was sitting next to her. Rosie and Stanley were sitting on the other side of the room. The cameras had been turned off and the microphones muted. The only thing keeping them from proceeding was Jeannine who was pacing the room.

"I don't know if I can do this," she said. "It was so frightening last time."

"But remember Jeannine, Mary will be with you," Ian said. "So, you don't have to be afraid."

"Do you promise, Mary, that you'll stay with me no matter what?"

Mary nodded. "I promise, I'll be there with you. Living it through you."

Jeannine took a deep breath. "Okay, let's do it before I chicken out."

Ian brought Mary under first, as he had the last time and then had her invite Jeannine in.

"Jeannine, where are you now?" he asked.

"I'm leaving Mary's room and walking," she said. "I really can't see much around me, but it's getting darker. I think I'm going back to the place where he kept me."

Mary could feel the temperature drop and she rubbed her hands against her arms. She was no longer walking. She was back on the rough couch in the dark room. Her mouth felt dry and her vision was slightly blurred, but she was feeling a little stronger than she had in the past. She stood up and wobbled a little. Bracing herself against the couch, she was amazed to find her pregnancy had progressed considerably.

"I'm really big now," Jeannine said. "I must be at least eight months pregnant. When the baby moves, my whole abdomen moves with her."

Mary placed her hand on her belly and felt the wonder of her baby. Moving her hands slowly, she could actually feel her baby beneath her skin. A rush of love and fierce protectiveness engulfed her. She had to get out of there. She had to save her baby.

Walking around the room, she searched for a window or a large vent, but the only door was the steel one that was always bolted. But was it always bolted or just when he wasn't down here with her?

She moved back over to the door and pulled on the latch. It was bolted shut. She looked at the hinges on the door and realized both the bolts and pins were on the other side. Her only chance, she decided, was to wait until he came downstairs and to catch him off guard.

This time when she looked around the room it was to find something she could use as a weapon against her captor. Lifting and discarding a number of items, she finally was able to find a loose cinder block in the corner of the room.

Half-dragging the block across the room, she paused when she heard the footfalls on the stairs. She knew she wouldn't make it to the door, so she carried it to the couch and hid it beneath her blanket.

The door burst open, just as she pulled the blanket over the block and her stomach.

"Darling, are you awake?" he asked. His voice was still slightly slurred, but it sounded familiar. If she could just concentrate for a little longer.

"I've been cutting down your drugs because we don't want to hurt the baby," he said. "But we don't want you to be too alert, do we? It's not as much fun when you're fighting me."

He sat on the edge of the couch and put his hands on her belly. "I can't tell you how much this excites me, darling," he said. "I love to see you swollen with my baby."

Her vision was still a little blurry, but she was beginning to focus on his face. It just needed to clear up a little more.

He bent forward and placed his head on her belly, next to his hands. "Come on, little girl," he cooed. "Let your daddy feel you move. Show your daddy how much you love him."

Anger and desperation gave her strength. She slid her hands under the blanket and picked up the cinder block. She pulled it out from under the blanket and swung it at his head with all her might.

"I hit him," Jeannine cried. "I hit him with the cinder block."

Jeannine's hand tightened on Ian's arm. "Oh, no," she cried. "I'm sorry. No, please, no!"

Jeannine's screams echoed in the room.

"You little bitch," he screamed, as he punched her in the face. "You ungrateful little bitch."

230

Mary could feel the pain echo through her jaw and into her head. She tried to protect herself from the next blow, but he grabbed her wrists and pulled them over her head as he punched her again and again. "No one does that to me," he screamed. "No one. Do you hear me?"

He dropped her wrists and the rest of her body fell with them against the couch. She could hear someone sobbing uncontrollably and realized it was her. She tried to touch her face, but the swelling had already begun and it was unrecognizable.

She felt the pinprick on her arm and the world started to fade away again. "I would have let you be without drugs," he said. "But you betrayed me. From now on, you will be so high, you won't know if you're awake or asleep."

And then her world went black.

Chapter Thirty-six

Mary was in pain. Sharp cramps had her nearly doubled over in agony. Her breath was coming out in gasps and her whole body hurt.

"Help me, please," she gasped.

The pain was gone for a moment. She reached out for her water glass. She was so thirsty. The cool water soothed her parched mouth and tongue. She didn't have much water left; the pains had been going on for at least an hour. Probably more, but she couldn't remember.

Another pain hit. She screamed. Oh, it hurt so much. Sweat poured from her face. Her whole body shuddered as she tried to control the pain. Then once again, the pain faded for the time being.

She heard footsteps and, for the first time, she welcomed them. The door opened. "Help me…" she started to say, then another fresh pain hit again. She screamed and pulled her legs up into a fetal position. Suddenly water exploded from her body and soaked the couch and her clothing.

"You're in labor," he yelled. "How long have you been having contractions?"

Mary looked up at him helplessly. "Help me, please," she said.

Then through her drug-induced haze she realized what he had said. "My baby," she said. "My baby. Help my baby."

He laid her back on the couch and stripped off her panties. She felt him press against her and she screamed. "Stop it," she screamed.

"This isn't supposed to be how it happened," he said, his voice rising in panic. "You were supposed to have a nice normal labor. There's something wrong here. Your baby isn't coming out the right way."

She reached out and grabbed his arm with her hand. "My baby," she cried, "save my baby."

"Wait here," he said. "I'll be right back."

"Don't leave me," Jeannine screamed, holding fast to Ian's arm. "You have to save my baby."

Mary's body was trembling uncontrollably by the time he got back to the room.

"Come on," he said. "We're going to a hospital."

He helped her up and bundled her into a blanket. She tried to climb the stairs, but her limbs were shaking too hard.

"Dammit, you're in transition," he said. "You're just going to have to hold on until we get there."

He helped her up the stairs, through the cold night air and into the back of the waiting car. She rolled back against the seat as he accelerated and she felt another contraction hit her body.

"Oh, my baby," Mary cried as the contraction wracked her body.

"Shut up," he screamed from the front seat. "Shut up or I'll pull this car over and you and your baby can die on a street corner."

She pulled the blanket up to her mouth and bit into it to muffle the sounds of labor. Tears streamed from her eyes as the contractions got closer together, but the drugs didn't allow her to brace herself for their impact.

The ride seemed to go on forever, but finally she felt him turn off the highway and drive down a street. She saw bright fluorescent lights just before the car door was opened. "Hurry, my wife, she's in labor," he called out.

Several people helped her out of the car and then they put her in a wheelchair. Her trembling had become worse and she was feeling nauseous.

"She's in transition," she heard someone say.

"She got into my drug supply," he said. "I think she took some Valium."

"No, my baby," Mary cried, trying to make them understand.

"Don't worry, honey," a comforting voice said. "We're gonna help you deliver that baby. I'm sorry, Dad, but you're gonna have to stay back in the waiting room. We got an emergency on our hands."

They wheeled her into a surgery room and lifted her up onto a bed. "Tell me, honey, how long have you been having these pains?" the nice voice said.

"A long time," Mary responded. "Hours."

"And how come you didn't come here sooner?"

"Locked up," she said. "Couldn't come."

"Yeah, you look a little rugged," she said. "Okay, now, I'm going to check you and see what the problem is with this little baby."

Mary bit her lip hard enough to bleed to stop crying out.

"Oh, honey, if you want to scream, you just go ahead and scream," the nice voice said.

"My baby," she whimpered.

"Oh, I think your baby is gonna be fine," she said. "She just got a little stuck, that's all."

Mary felt more pressure and took a deep breath.

"That's it honey, take a couple more of those deep breaths."

Suddenly she needed to push down. "Oh, there you go girl," the voice said. "You know what to do."

"Okay, now, that contraction's over, so you take it easy and suck on these ice chips."

"Thank you," Mary whispered.

"Oh, honey, you don't need to thank me," she said. "But you call me, anytime you need anything. My name is Rachael."

"Thank you, Rachael," Mary stammered.

"There you go, thanking me again," the doctor said. "You got a name I can call you?"

"No, owwwwww," she moaned as the next contraction hit.

"Okay, honey, I see a head coming out," Rachael said. "Someone get me a baby kit and one 1 mL of Syntometrine in case she's a bleeder."

"No," Mary panted. "No shot."

"Oh, honey, don't worry," Rachael said. "I won't give it to you until the baby is almost out. It helps prevent hemorrhaging and you can't lose any more blood."

"No," Mary panted.

"Okay honey, bear down and push that baby out."

Mary pushed down with all her might, felt the whoosh of the baby slip from her body and then she felt the pinprick in her side. She heard the sound of her baby's cry and tried to lift her arms to hold her. But suddenly she couldn't breathe.

"We got a Code Blue in here," Rachael called. "Code Blue. Get in here right now."

"I can't breathe," Jeannine screamed. "Help me. I…I…I can't."

Her hand went limp on Ian's arm.

"Jeannine," he called. "Jeannine come back."

Mary's face was pale and drawn. "Mary! Mary can you hear me?"

Stanley and Rosie rushed over to the couch.

"Mary, I need you to respond. I need you to come back," he said. "We need you here. Your job's not done here. You have to still find the baby."

Mary's body shuddered. "Ian," she said.

Ian ran his hand over her forehead. "Oh, God," he breathed softly, tears in his eyes. "Yes sweetheart, you can hear me?"

"Ian, the baby," she said. "I can't find the baby."

"The baby is somewhere in this world Mary," he said. "You have to come home and then we can all find it."

"It hurt, Ian," she whispered.

"Oh, darling, I'm sure it did," he said. "And you were so brave. I was so proud of you."

"Ian, I see my room," she said. "I'm so tired. Can I take a nap?"

"Well, you can take a short nap in your room and then when I bring you home, you can nap for the rest of the day. Okay?"

She nodded her head. "Okay."

"Now, Mary, lie down on the couch and close your eyes," he said. "Close your eyes and take a nap. Are you sleeping, Mary?"

She nodded again, slowly.

"Mary, darling, I want you to wake up and be back with us," he said.

Mary opened her eyes and they immediately filled with tears. Rosie bent down and embraced Mary in her arms. Mary didn't try to be brave or strong this time. All she wanted to do was cry for Jeannine.

Chapter Thirty-seven

An hour later, Mary had taken a hot shower and put on her Chicago Police Department sweats and wool socks and was seated at the dining room table placing a video call to Sean.

"Hey, sis, you look like you had a rough night," he said as he greeted her.

"You always know how to cheer a woman's heart, Sean," she replied.

"And that's why I'm not married."

"Truer words were never spoken, Sean,"

"So, what can I do for you?" he asked.

"I've got some information on Jeannine's death and I'd like you to follow up on it," she explained.

"Sure, what do you have?"

"She was in labor and I'm pretty sure she was taken to Cook County Hospital," Mary explained, "which would make sense, because that's where we picked up her ghost, after Bradley was taken there with a gunshot wound."

"Yeah, that's right," he said. "Okay, Cook County."

"The doctor's name was Rachael; she performed an emergency delivery that came in sometime during the night. The pregnant woman was high on something," she said. "She received an

238

injection, I think it was Syntometrine, after the baby was born. She had a bad reaction. The woman died of cardiac arrest."

"Damn," Sean said sadly. "What happened to Bradley's baby?"

"I don't know," Mary replied. "I'm hoping you can find that out too."

"So how much are you telling Bradley at this point?" he asked.

"Nothing yet," she said. "Not until I have some solid evidence for him. He doesn't need any more false leads."

"You're right," he said. "You're doing a fine job, Mary. You and that motley crew of yours."

Mary laughed. "They've been exactly what we needed to solve this case, Sean. Ian has been invaluable."

"I'll make sure it's part of his record when I put it together."

"Thanks. Have you received any feedback on any of the subjects yet?"

"No, I'll have it for you after your brunch," he said. "So, once you say your goodbyes I'll get online and we can go through all of the information."

"Perfect," she said. "Thanks Sean. Love you."

"Love you too," he said. "Talk to you tomorrow."

Mary started toward the kitchen, but at the foot of the stairs she heard a sound that made her pause. Someone was crying.

She ran upstairs and followed the sound to the nursery at the end of the hall. She opened the door and found Jeannine sitting in the rocking chair, holding a baby blanket in her arms and sobbing.

As Mary entered the room, Jeannine looked up at her. "I didn't even get to hold her," she said. "I could hear her crying for me. My heart was aching. I tried to lift my arms."

She bowed her head and wept some more.

Mary closed the door and sat on the floor next to the chair. "I don't know what to say. There are no words for what happened to you, what that man did to you."

"Will you find him?" she asked.

Mary nodded. "Yes, I will find him. I promise you."

"Will you find my baby?" she pleaded, her lips quivering with emotion.

Wiping her owns tears away, she nodded. "Yes, I will find your daughter and I'll make sure she knows all about her wonderful, brave mother."

"You felt it, didn't you?"

"Felt it?

"You felt me give birth," Jeannine said. "You felt the pain."

"And the joy," Mary said, "at the end."

"Yes, there was joy, wasn't there?" she said. "I remember hearing her cry. It was like angels were in the room."

"You saved your baby, Jeannine. You gave that little girl life. She will be yours forever."

"Thank you for helping me remember, Mary," she said. "I'll always be grateful to you."

Mary covered her mouth to hold back the sobs. "You're welcome, Jeannine," she whispered through her tears as she watched Jeannine fade away.

Chapter Thirty-eight

"Stanley, stop snacking on the muffins," Rosie said, as she pulled a pan of breakfast casserole out of the oven. "Or there won't be any left for the guests."

"Bunch of no-good murderers," Stanley muttered, propping himself on one of the stools near the island. "They don't deserve your muffins."

"Now Stanley, not all of them are murderers," Rosie reminded him. "Only one of them is."

"Yes, the rest are just plain nuts," he replied. "Don't know why we have to feed them."

"Because that's what you do at a brunch, Stanley," Mary said, as she picked up the silverware and napkins. "The table is almost set Rosie. What else can I do?"

"Just make sure Ian has all of his computer controls out of the way," she said. "It makes such an unsightly mess."

Mary grinned. "I'll have him put a tablecloth over it."

Rosie turned abruptly. "Mary!"

"Just teasing, Rosie, I'll have him tidy it up."

Mary laid the cutlery and linens at the end of the buffet, next to the plates. She looked around at the various dishes already lined up, ready to be served. Once again, Rosie had outdone herself. She only wished her stomach was not so tied up in knots that it would prevent her from enjoying any of the food.

"Good morning, wifey dear," Ian said. "How are the preparations going?"

"Rosie is cooking up a storm, Stanley is complaining and Rosie is chastising him," she said.

"Ach, a typical meal at the MacDougal castle," he said with a grin. "And may I add that the mistress of the castle looks delectable herself. I like the white frothy thing."

Mary looked down at her loose flowing white peasant-style blouse. "Thanks, I thought it gave me a 'remember I'm expecting' sort of look."

"Sorry, no," Ian said. "It gives you a sort of a fairy-tale come hither look. Quite sexy."

"And look at you," she said, noting his black cotton Henley shirt and jeans. "You look pretty good yourself."

"I put on a tighter fitting shirt for the occasion," he said. "But after we're done, the boys go back in hiding."

"A sad day for womankind everywhere," she teased. "By the way, Rosie sent me to make sure you've cleaned up your mess of computer equipment."

Ian grinned. "Aye, I've hidden it all in the closet. Isn't that what you're supposed to do when your mother asks you to clean your room?"

Mary nodded. "It's a requirement."

The doorbell rang and Mary placed her hand over her stomach. "Showtime," she said.

"Aye, let's get 'em."

Mercedes and Harvey were the first to arrive.

"Hello, Professor MacDougal," she said. "Or may I call you Ian?"

"Ian will be fine," he said. "It's not likely that you'd be one of my students."

She smiled. "Oh, I'm sure there are plenty of things you could teach me."

Mary's eyes widened. The woman had no tact at all; Mary was standing within three feet of Ian. "Did Ian happen to mention what he teaches?" she asked Mercedes.

Shaking her head, Mercedes smiled coyly. "Ancient Scottish history?"

"Oh, no, I teach paranormal psychology," he said. "The study of things beyond our basic five senses."

"You mean things like ghosts?" Mercedes asked.

"Aye, exactly."

"And the funniest thing," Mary said. "It seems we have a ghost here in this house. Ian's seen her a couple of times."

"Aye, a pretty young woman," Ian said. "She seems to walk between the kitchen and the dining room."

"Tell them the funniest part, dear," Mary said.

"Oh, no, I insist, you do it, darling," Ian said, wondering what in the world Mary was doing.

244

"She's looking for a basket of muffins," Mary laughed. "Can you believe it?"

Mercedes's face turned pale and she dropped her purse on the ground. "A basket of muffins?"

"Aye," Ian responded. "I'm hoping to hold a séance in the next couple of days to see if I can get more information from her. It would be interesting to see if someone actually stole a basket of muffins from her."

Mercedes nodded slowly. "Yes, it would be very interesting."

"Muffins anyone?" Rosie called out, holding a basket in her hands. "They're a special kind of bran muffin. For some reason a little voice kept telling me to make them."

Mary turned to Mercedes and Harvey. "Do you like bran muffins?" she asked.

Mercedes stepped away from Mary, taking her husband with her. "I think I need to sit down for a while."

"That went quite well," Ian whispered to Mary.

"Yes, I think it did too."

"Muffin?" he asked, handing her one from the basket.

She grinned. "Don't mind if I do."

The doorbell rang again and both Bob and Gary were standing on the doorstep together.

"So, do you believe that extraterrestrials can actually read our thoughts by using the metals in our fillings?" Bob asked Gary.

"Well, Bob, that's something I never considered," he replied. "But let me do some research into that and I'll get back to you."

Gary turned and saw Mary at the door. "Please come in out of the cold," she said.

"Hello, Mary, how are you feeling today?" Gary asked as he stepped inside the house.

"Oh, much better, thank you," she said. "It was so kind of you to help me."

Ian walked up behind her and put his arm around her shoulders. "Aye, we both owe you a debt of thanks," he said. "I couldn't go on if something happened to her."

"Mary you look so pretty today," Bob said. "Like a bride."

"Thank you, Bob, that was very sweet," she replied.

Rosie appeared next to them. "Hello, Bob, how are you today?"

"Just fine, Rosie, everything smells so delicious."

Rosie turned to Gary. "You must be Gary," she said. "I don't think we've met. I'm Rosie, Mary's grandmother."

"Oh, you must be lying," he said.

Rosie's face turned pale and she looked at Mary in panic. "Mary, what should I say?" she asked.

"Oh, I'm sorry," Gary said. "I was only teasing. I thought you looked far too young to be Mary's grandmother."

"Oh," Rosie said, breathing a sigh of relief. "I thought you meant that I was actually lying and I do so hate to lie. I only do it in the most extreme circumstances."

"Care to expand on what those circumstances might be, sweetie?" Stanley asked.

"Oh, Stanley," Rosie said, blushing. "You are such a tease."

"Why don't we all go into the dining room?" Mary suggested. "I think brunch is almost ready to be served."

"Yes, do go," Rosie insisted. "I'll have the rest of the dishes out in a minute."

Most of the group left, but Gary remained behind. "Rosie, I really need to apologize for my comment," he said. "I'm not very good with people, so I often end up putting my foot in my mouth."

Rosie stepped forward and put her hand on his arm. "Oh, no, it was nothing," she said. "Really."

"Well, would you please allow me to help you carry these dishes in to make up for it?" he asked. "I would feel so much better."

Smiling Rosie nodded. "Of course, you can."

"Why don't I carry in the pitchers of drinks?" he offered.

"That would be lovely," she said, picking up a plate of fruit.

He lifted the pitchers and then said. "Oh, these have condensation on the bottom. Let me wipe them off and I'll join you directly."

"Well, thank you, Gary," she said. "Most men wouldn't understand what a mess condensation can make in a table setting."

Once Rosie left the room, Gary slipped the packets of powder out of his pocket and mixed it into the pitchers of juice. "And most men aren't me, Rosie."

Chapter Thirty-nine

"When is their party going to end?" Sean wondered, as he sat at his desk waiting for the follow up call. The computers had gone down in his area, so he hadn't been able to watch the brunch via the camera hook-up, but he figured Mary would call once the party was over. Finally, frustrated, he called Bradley to see if he had been watching.

"Chief Alden," Bradley said when he answered his cell phone. "Hi, Sean, what's up?"

"Have you been watching the Mary and Ian show lately?" Sean asked.

He walked over to his computer and turned it on. "No," he said. "I haven't kept tabs on them today. I figured you were watching, so I could get some work done."

Typing in his password, he pressed enter and waited for his screen to appear. "Weren't you supposed to have a meeting with them after the brunch?" he asked.

"Yeah," Sean replied. "I figured the brunch would be finished in a couple of hours at the most. It's been nearly three hours and, I hate to admit it, I'm a little concerned."

"Okay, I got the link," Bradley said. "It's taking a few moments to load."

The video links came up and Bradley clicked on each room to get a closer look. There was no one in the kitchen, no one in the front room, no one in the dining…wait!

"Sean, I got a view of the dining room and it looks like everyone is asleep at the table," he said.

"What the hell?" Sean asked. "Is Mary there?"

Bradley zoomed in, went around the table and his heart sunk. "No, Sean, I don't see her," he said.

"Okay, well, she could be in one of the bathrooms," Sean said.

"I'm going," Bradley said. "I can be there in less than an hour."

"Call me when you get there," Sean said. "I'll be heading out as soon as I can."

Bradley ran to his cruiser, flipped on the siren and headed out to Highway 20. He put a call through to his former police chief in Sycamore.

"Hey, Chief, this is Bradley Alden. I got a problem at my old house. I've got some friends staying there and I can't get hold of any of them. I'm a little concerned something might have happened to them. Could you have someone go by and check it out?"

"Is this related to what happened eight years ago?" his former chief asked.

"Yeah, I'm afraid it might be," Bradley said. "And it could literally be a case of life or death."

"I'll head over there myself," he said. "I still got a copy of your house key."

"Thanks, I'm on my way too. I should be there in about forty-five minutes."

"I'll call you when I get there," the chief said. "And let you know what's going on."

"Thanks again."

Sean picked up the files from his secretary and started down the hallway of the downtown police station. He was almost to the elevator when someone shouted his name.

"Hey, Sean, wait."

Sean turned to see one of the newer recruits jogging down the hall toward him. "This just came in from Cook County and your secretary thought you might want it."

Sean scanned the pages of the fax. The doctor had indeed remembered the case and she was able to put her hands on the death certificate right away. The woman that had died that night during labor had been identified by her husband as Beverly Copper.

"Thanks, I appreciate it," he said to the recruit just as the elevator opened. "Hey, find out where they buried her."

Chapter Forty

Chief Kip Vitner was at the Alden place within five minutes of the call. He hurried up the walkway, key in hand, but found the door standing open. He reached into his holster for his service revolver and slowly entered the house.

He moved through the hallway, his back against the wall, and peered into the living room. It was empty. Then he moved on to the dining room and caught his breath. There were bodies scattered all over the room. He holstered his gun and moved forward. The first body was that of an older woman. She was laying with her head on the table and her hand touching the elderly man by her side. Kip reached over and placed his fingertips at the base of her neck. She still had a pulse.

Pulling out his radio, he called for back-up and ambulances.

He moved around the table and found that all of the victims were still alive. However, there were two empty place settings.

A moment later, several uniformed police officers entered the house. "I want you to check the rest of the house," he said. "We're missing two people."

The young man at the end of the table began to stir. He lifted his head. "What happened?" he asked.

"It looks like you were drugged."

He stood up, his knees nearly buckling beneath him, but he caught himself and forced his muscles to hold him. "Where's Mary?" he gasped.

"Who?"

"Mary O'Reilly," he yelled. "Where the hell is Mary?"

"Hey, listen, buddy," Kip said, moving toward Ian. "You and your friends have been drugged up pretty bad. And it looks like some of your party is missing."

Ian shoved away from the table and moved to the base of the stairs. "Mary," he called.

"Hey, listen, buddy, I've got officers up there searching all the rooms," he said. "If your Mary is in this house we'll find her."

"I've got to call Bradley," Ian said.

"He's on his way," Kip replied. "He's the one who called me. He'll be here in less than 30 minutes."

"I pray that's quick enough," he said.

Just then Jeannine appeared behind Kip. "Ian, what happened?"

Ian, still feeling the effects of the drug, forgot that no one else could see Jeannine.

"Oh, thank the Lord, you've come," he said. "They've taken Mary."

"Yeah, I know that," Kip said. "I told you."

"Who took her?" Jeannine asked.

Ian shook his head. "I don't know," he said. "Who is still here at the party?"

"I don't know who's at your party," Kip replied.

"I'm not talking to you, man," Ian said. "I'm talking to the ghost."

"Okay, buddy, you just stand there and have your little trip and I'll look after the others."

Jeannine floated around the room. "I see Bob, Mercedes and Harvey," she said, "and Rosie and Stanley. Who's missing?"

"Gary," Ian said. "The one everyone trusted. Gary has her."

"Gary was the one who took me?" Jeannine asked. "Gary did this to me?"

Ian nodded. "It looks that way," he said.

"Is he going to do to her what he did to me?"

Ian recalled the horrors he recorded while Jeannine was being hypnotized. "I hope not."

"Can you go to her, Jeannine?" he asked. "Just to give her comfort."

Jeannine nodded. "I'll go," she said. "I won't let him hurt Mary."

Jeannine faded away and Ian turned back to Kip. "I know who has Mary," he said. "You need to send some officers over to Dr. Gary Copper's home."

"You got some proof he did this?" Kip asked. "Dr. Copper is very well-known and trusted in this community. I can't break into his house without proof."

"Please, she could be in trouble," Ian said. "There's no time to waste."

"Listen, I don't know how things are handled where you come from, but here in the United States of America people are innocent until proven guilty. You get me some evidence and I'll obtain a warrant."

Bradley was already on Highway 39 heading south toward Sycamore when the call back from Kip came. "The good news is they're all alive," he said. "The bad news is they're pretty messed up. And the foreign guy refuses to go to the hospital. Says he needs to run the tapes for you. But he can barely walk, much less run anything."

"Is there a young woman there? Her name is Mary."

"No, she's not here," Kip said. "That foreign guy's been through every room in the house, calling her name."

"How bad is Ian, the foreign guy?" Bradley asked.

"He's moving around better than the rest of them. He looks like maybe he didn't ingest as much as the others. But the safe thing would be to take him to the hospital."

"Let him stay," Bradley said. "I'll be there in about fifteen minutes and I could really use his help."

"He wants to talk to you," Kip said. "But he's pretty strung out; he's been talking to ghosts."

"Put him on."

"Bradley, it's Gary, he's got Mary," Ian said.

"That can't be right," Bradley said. "He was our friend. I always trusted him."

"It's got to be Gary," Ian said. "The rest of the suspects are here. Jeannine's gone to be with Mary. But if he's the one... The things he did to Jeannine... We've got to get to Mary right away."

"Ask Kip..."

"I've already asked your friend, the chief," he said. "He's not moving unless we have proof. Even if I have film of Mary leaving with Gary, it probably won't show her leaving under duress."

"I'll go straight to his house," Bradley said. "You stay at the house and wait for Sean."

"Hurry, Bradley," Ian said.

Chapter Forty-one

The room was dark and damp and Mary recognized it at once. This was the place Jeannine had been kept. She moved her hand along the rough texture of the couch. She remembered that too. She could smell the mold, but there was another scent mixing with it. Her vision was still blurry and her body was sluggish and slow to respond. But she was able to turn her head slowly.

Candles.

Tall white candles were standing on a table in the corner of the room. She didn't remember candles from before.

"Ian," she called out. "Ian, I don't want to do this anymore."

She looked down at herself and saw the white blouse she'd put on that morning. These weren't Jeannine's clothes. "Ian, bring me home."

"But darling, you are home."

Mary felt nausea rise in her throat and she shook her head in disbelief. "No, this isn't happening," she whimpered. "Please this can't be happening to me."

She struggled to move back into the corner of the couch.

"You just make yourself comfortable darling," he said. "And I'll put on a little soothing music."

The soft sounds of "Make it With You" drifted through the room. "They're playing our song, Mary," he said. "Don't you want to dance with me?"

She shook her head. "No, please, just let me go home."

"Oh, baby," he said, moving up next to her and stroking his hand lightly up and down her arm. "Sooner or later you and I are going to get to know each other in, shall I say, an intimate way. You might as well decide to like it."

Mary shuddered. "You killed Jeannine," she said. "You kept her here and then you killed her."

Gary grabbed her arm tightly and squeezed. "How did you know that?"

"I saw what you did," Mary said, trying to twist away from him. "I saw how you touched her. You are not going to touch me that way."

"Oh, that's what you think," he said.

He crossed the room and picked up a hypodermic needle. "I just need to make you a little more agreeable," he said. "This is what we like to call a twilight drug – your mind goes to sleep, but your body is delightfully awake."

Grabbing her arm once again, he thrust the needle into her bicep and pushed down on the syringe. "There, in a few minutes you're going to enjoy this as much as I will."

He grabbed her wrists in one hand and pulled them over her head. Then he climbed over her, straddling her hips. "Now, try and stop me," he said, sliding his hand beneath her shirt and slowly making his way up.

Mary tried to buck him off, but he had her pinned down into the cushions of the couch.

"Your skin is like silk," he murmured. "I can't wait to taste all of it."

Mary shivered with revulsion and turned her head away.

"Oh, darling, don't you want to watch what I do to you?" he asked.

He removed his hand from under her shirt and clasped her chin to force her head forward. He bent forward and kissed her, exploring her face with small licks of his tongue. "Oh, yes, you do taste delicious, just as I thought."

Suddenly one of the candles tipped over and fell on the floor. "Damn," he said, looking up across the room. He released her hands and climbed off of her.

"Don't move," he added with a smirk.

"Mary, I'm here," Jeannine said appearing next to her.

Tears flowed down Mary's face. "I don't want to die," she whispered. "I can't move my body."

"Yeah, I know, he's got you drugged."

Jeannine looked over and saw that Gary was taking the time to relight the candles. She quickly glided over and knocked the other one down.

"Okay," she said when she got back. "Remember what Ian said about spirits taking over your body when you're drunk? Well, I think that drugged must be pretty much the same. Right?"

Mary nodded.

"So, can I try and help you?" she asked. "Using your body and my spirit?"

"I can't help you," she whispered. "Everything is starting to go black again."

"It's okay," Jeannine said. "Your body already knows some awesome moves. But instead of you, I'm going to drive."

"Well, we have candlelight again, darling," he said. "Have you ever made love by candlelight?"

"Have you ever had your ass kicked by candlelight?" Jeannine asked, and then she entered Mary's body.

She watched him as he moved closer. She knew she only had one shot at surprise and it was going to be a good one.

"Now, where were we?" he asked and lifted his leg to climb over Mary.

Jeannine placed her first kick right between his legs and sent him sprawling off the couch, clutching his crotch.

Jeannine got up from the couch and came toward him.

"But you're drugged," he wheezed.

"Oh, my good friend Mary is drugged," she said. "But this time, Gary boy, you're dealing with Jeannine Alden."

She kicked him in the stomach and then again in his side.

"But you're dead!"

"You don't think I'm pissed enough?" she yelled. "You want to remind me?"

He struggled to his feet. "You can try to fight me, but I'm stronger than you."

She realized she didn't really know how to do any of the karate moves Mary had been trained in. *Oh well*, she thought, *I can improvise.*

She lifted her hands over her head and then lifted one leg up and bent it.

"What the hell are you doing?" Gary asked.

"Karate kid," Jeannine said, jumping forward and catching Gary directly in the chest with the kick.

He flew backward into the table and lay sprawled on the floor.

Jeannine picked up a broom handle, carried it across the room, and shoved it against Gary's throat. "What did you do to my body?" she asked.

"I buried it," he said. "Using Beverly's name. I buried you in a grave at Resurrection Cemetery."

"Where's my baby?" she asked, pushing the handle further down.

He gagged. "I don't know," he gasped. "I told Child Services to take her. Told them I couldn't deal with her. Told them I wasn't the father."

261

Chapter Forty-two

Bradley tore down the residential street and pulled up to the front door of Gary's house. He pulled the "jaws of life" tool out of the back seat of his car and made his way to the door. With a quick check, he found the door locked. And with a quick swing of his tool, the door was hanging open.

The house was quiet and felt deserted, but he needed to check every room, just in case. He hurried down the front hall, looking into each room he passed. Not only was there no one in the rooms, each of the rooms had an unlived feel. Like someone put furniture in there for show, but never used the rooms.

After a thorough search, he knew there was no one on the first floor. He ran to the staircase and took the stairs three at a time. The first door he opened was a guest room that had the same unused look as the room downstairs.

He hurried to the next door. Opening it, he inhaled sharply. It was a nursery, painted in pink and white. There was a crib in the corner with a pink satin comforter, crib bumper and even one small pillow. It was the same set he and Jeannine had purchased for their baby, but, he recalled absently, they had two small pillows.

The next room was the master bedroom. Bradley entered the large room and hurried over to the walk in closet. He opened the door and was shocked by his discovery. The entire wall was covered with the bits and pieces of photos of Jeannine that had been stolen from his home during the break-in. He had made a collage of her, along with newspaper articles about her disappearance.

Bradley was about to leave the closet when he noticed something on the other wall. He shoved aside the hung clothing and revealed the beginnings of another collage. This one featured Mary. There were photos taken of her in the master bedroom of Bradley's house by what looked like a long-range telephoto lens, as well as candid shots of her outside the house.

A cold chill ran down his spine. He had to find her as soon as possible.

He ran down the stairs and back through the kitchen to the basement door. He hurried down the stairs, oblivious to any danger he might be facing. He only wanted to find Mary.

Stopping at the bottom of the stairs, he scanned the room. It was nearly empty. All he saw was a furnace, water heater and some shelves with old paint cans. He moved closer to the shelving. Something wasn't right there.

He looked at the floor and saw the gray concrete paint had scrape marks on it, but there was nothing around that could make the marks. Then he realized the house lines in the basement didn't match up with the rest of the house. He walked to the edge of the shelf and pushed. It moved forward. Pushing against it harder, it slid forward and revealed a steel door. Surprised to find it unlocked, he pushed it open and moved inside.

Pulling a flashlight from his belt, he slowly scanned the dark room. In one corner were a small table and a folding chair. In another corner, he could see a white door.

He moved into the room, focusing on the door in the corner. As he came closer, he saw it was the door to a freezer, but he'd seen enough cases where doors like these were used to camouflage a real doorway. Pulling it open, he peered inside.

The light from the freezer shone brightly into the dark room and it took Bradley's eyes a moment to adjust. And then he saw her.

All of his worst nightmares came true as he stared at what must have been Jeannine's frozen mutilated body. He turned away from the freezer and took several deep breaths, trying to halt his gag reflex. Then he forced himself to turned back and examine the body.

He bent down on the floor and tried to distance himself from the horror that was screaming inside his mind. He could see her legs had been removed from her torso, so she could fit upright in the freezer. *They must be stored on the upper shelf,* he thought.

He stood up to catalog the items on the shelf and found the little white box. His heart dropped. With shaking hands he slowly lifted the lid. The tiny frozen embryo lay wrapped in plastic, huddled on a pink satin pillow. He clutched the box to his chest, fell to his knees and cried.

The blaring tone of his cell phone echoed in the room. Bradley pulled it from his pocket. "Yes," he answered, his voice rough with emotion.

"It's Sean. I wanted you to know that Copper buried Jeannine in a cemetery in Chicago," he said. "I'm working on exhumation orders."

"Are you sure?"

"Yeah, he brought her into Cook County, she died there," he said.

Bradley looked more closely at the body in the freezer and realized it was Beverly Copper, Gary's first wife.

"But, Bradley, we don't know where the baby is."

He sealed up the little box and placed it back in the freezer. "I think I do," he said, wiping away his tears. He could mourn for his daughter later. Now he had to find Mary.

"Listen, Gary isn't here at his house," he continued. "The only other place he could be is at his office in downtown Sycamore. I'm headed there now."

"Okay, I'm only a few minutes out, I'll meet you there," Sean said.

Chapter Forty-three

Jeannine gasped. "My baby is alive?"

Gary took that moment to grab the broom handle and pull it from her hands. He whipped it around and rammed it into her legs. Jeannine stumbled backward and Gary pounced.

He lifted his hand to punch her, but she feinted to the side and he missed her. She lifted her leg and caught him in the gut with her knee. Then she elbowed him in the neck and rolled out from beneath him.

She scrambled across the floor, and then jumped up, putting the couch between them.

He picked up the broom handle and walked toward her. "I never meant to hurt you," he said.

"You killed me, you son-of-a-bitch," Jeannine said.

"I didn't kill you," he said, stopping on the other side of the couch. "It was the hospital, they made the mistake. I didn't."

"You told them I was your wife," she replied. "They didn't have my medical records; they didn't know I was allergic to that drug. When you lied to them about who I was, you killed me."

He slapped the broomstick against his hand. "You women are all alike," he said. "Always blaming me. Beverly blamed me because the women I worked on wanted me. It wasn't my fault."

"They wanted you?" Jeannine asked.

"She found the videos I took," he said. "I tried to tell her they liked it. They wanted me. They were drugged because they didn't want to feel guilty."

Jeannine shook her head. "You are one sick creep," she said. "No wonder Beverly left you."

He shook his head and chuckled. "Oh, she didn't leave me," he said. "She's still at home waiting for me. Just like you are going to wait for me."

"Like hell she is," Bradley yelled from the open doorway, before he lunged at Gary.

Bradley punched him in the jaw and knocked him backward. Then he grabbed him by the collar and rammed his head into the concrete wall. "You killed my wife," he screamed, knocking his head against the wall again.

"You killed my child," he screamed, knocking him again.

"You will never, ever, do that to anyone else," he said, knocking him against the wall once more.

"Bradley, stop," Jeannine yelled. "You're going to kill him."

"Good," Bradley growled through clenched teeth. "He doesn't deserve to live."

"Bradley, stop." Jeannine grabbed on to his arm and tried to pull him away.

Suddenly a strong pair of arms moved Jeannine to the side and pulled Bradley off the unconscious, badly battered man. "Alden, control yourself," Sean said. "This isn't the way and you know it."

Bradley stepped back and took a shuddering gasp when he looked at Gary's bloody face.

"I wanted to kill him," he said, his voice a combination of disbelief and regret.

"Yeah, I get that," Sean said. "But you didn't and that's what matters."

Bradley met Sean's gaze and nodded. "Thanks."

"I'll wait here for the paramedics," Sean said. "Why don't you take Mary upstairs to the waiting room?"

Bradley turned around. "Mary, are you all right?" he asked.

"I am, now that you're here," she said.

He scooped her up in his arms and carried her to the small waiting room at the top of the stairs. He placed her on her feet and cradled her head in his hands.

"Bradley, you need to know something before you kiss me," she whispered.

He lowered his face. "Anything we need to discuss can wait."

"Bradley, I'm not Mary, I'm Jeannine."

Bradley froze and lifted his head. "No, you're Mary," he said. "I was married to Jeannine, I know the difference."

Jeannine laughed. "No, I mean that I'm inside Mary's body," she said. "It was the only way to save her, because Gary had drugged her."

268

Bradley shook his head. "You're serious? Jeannine?"

She smiled at him. "Takes a while to get through that thick skull of yours, but you finally do catch on."

"You saved Mary?" he asked.

"Yeah," she said with a smile. "I really like her. So don't do anything stupid and mess it up."

He chuckled. "Well, I've tried pretty much every stupid thing I can think of. I hope I can start being smarter soon."

She laid her head on his chest. "I really do love you, you know," she said.

He hugged her close and kissed her hair. "And I love you."

She looked up at him, her eyes bright with tears. "I don't think Mary would mind," she said, as she wrapped her arms around him and kissed him for one last time.

She stepped out of Mary's body and Mary collapsed into Bradley's arms. He looked out and saw Jeannine's ghost standing in front of them. "I get to go home now, Bradley," she said. "Promise me…"

"Anything," he said, cradling Mary's body in his arms.

"Find my body and put me in a proper grave. And find our baby."

Bradley thought about the tiny body in the freezer across town. Jeannine didn't need to know what happened to their baby. She needed to rest in peace. "I will, Jeannine, I promise."

"Goodbye, Bradley," she said, as she faded away. "Take good care of Mary."

"Goodbye, Jeannine," he whispered to the empty room.

Chapter Forty-four

Bradley sat vigil at Mary's bedside in the hospital in Freeport. He knew she didn't like hospitals and wanted to be sure that he was there when she finally woke up.

Dr. Louise Thorne had examined her when she came in and said that until the drug wore off, they wouldn't know if any other injuries had occurred. That was two days ago and everyone, including Dr. Thorne, was getting a little worried.

He looked around the room and had to smile. This place had more stuff in it than the gift shop. There were half a dozen bouquets of flowers from red roses to yellow daisies. There were boxes of chocolates, dozens of cards, a goldfish in a goblet from the Brennan boys and several plates of cookies and baked goods from Rosie.

He got up and picked up a cookie from one of the plates and bit into it.

"Filching cookies from an invalid," Mike said. "That's pretty low."

"She's not an invalid, she just hasn't woken up yet," Bradley said. "And Rosie said Mary could share."

Mike glided over to Mary. "Did you ever wonder if that fairy tale thing worked?" he asked. "You lean over and kiss her and she opens her eyes."

"Well, I could run it past Dr. Thorne and see what she thinks," Bradley said.

"Skeptic," Mike countered.

"Hey, I've been meaning to talk to you," Bradley said. "About that issue we had before I went into Sycamore."

"Yeah, did you make a decision?"

Bradley nodded. "I called Jack and told him that I was going to have to follow up on the case," he said, watching Mike's expression fall. "But given my case load and the fact that the insurance companies paid for all of the damages to the farmers, and since there was no viable forensic evidence, the investigation was going to have to be tabled for about eighteen months."

Mike smiled. "You're a good man, Bradley Alden."

He shook his head. "No, I just got a peek of how people react when their loved ones have been hurt by someone else."

"So, training and civility don't always win?"

"No, they should, Mike, they really should, but there's something primitive inside us that fights for release," he said. "And if we're not careful, we can rationalize that it's right."

"Are you saying that what Jack did was wrong?"

Bradley nodded. "Yeah, what he did was wrong. Because once we start taking justice into our own hands, once we think we have the right to decide who gets to live and who gets to die, we've lost our ability to exist as a civilized society."

"So, why give Jack a break?"

Bradley smiled sadly. "Because, this time, whether justice works swiftly or slowly, the results will be the same."

"Thanks anyway, Bradley," he said as he started to fade away.

"You're welcome," Bradley said.

There was a soft knock on the door and Bradley turned to see Rosie and Stanley entering the room. "Is she awake yet?" Rosie asked.

Bradley shook his head. "No, not yet."

"Oh, dear," Rosie said. "We wanted to share our news with her."

"Your news?" Bradley asked.

Rosie smiled. "Stanley's asked me to marry him."

"Well, you've tasted her cooking," Stanley grumbled. "A man would be a fool not to snatch her up."

Rosie giggled. "Come on, Stanley, tell him what you told me."

"Darn demanding women," he grumbled. "Fine, I'll tell you, but don't go spreading it around. People are going think I've gone and gotten soft."

"I promise," Bradley said.

Stanley walked over to Rosie and took her hand in his. "At our age we don't have too much time left, so we can't waste any chances we get. Iffen you find someone who makes your world a better place, you got to snatch her up and spend all the time you can with her."

Rosie wiped a tear from her eye. "He meant me," she explained to Bradley.

"Yeah, I kind of got that," he said with a chuckle. "And he's not only lucky, he's a smart man."

Rosie blushed. "Thank you, Bradley."

"So, when's the date?" he asked.

"Oh, we can't settle on that until Mary's awake," Rosie said. "She's got to be my maid-of-honor."

Stanley harrumphed. "And I'd be pleased if you'd be my best man."

"Stanley, I'd be honored," Bradley said sincerely.

Stanley nodded his head. "Well, good, thanks," he said, pulling out his handkerchief and wiping his nose. "Appreciate it."

Rosie slipped her arm through Stanley's and sighed. "It's like a fairy tale come true," she said.

"Yeah, who'd every guess the troll would get the princess," Stanley said, his eyes filled with love for Rosie.

Rosie leaned over and kissed Stanley. "I've always had a particular fondness for trolls."

Stanley blushed. "Well, we'd best be going," he said. "You call us when she wakes up, hear?"

Bradley nodded. "Yes, you're at the top of the list."

"Thank you, Bradley," Rosie said, leaning over and kissing him on the cheek.

"My pleasure, Rosie."

They left the room and Bradley turned back to Mary, still sleeping soundly. He walked over to the bed and looked down at her. She did look like a fairy-tale princess, lying there magically asleep. He wondered if…?

He started to lean over toward her when he heard a sharp rap on the door.

"It's a sick room, Sean," Ian was saying. "You don't enter it like you do a pub."

"I didn't mean to knock so hard," he said, walking into the room. "I didn't wake her up, did I?"

Bradley shook his head. "No, she's still asleep."

Ian walked up to the bed, bent over and was going to kiss Mary.

"Wait," Bradley said, panicked.

Ian looked up and grinned. "Ach, don't worry, it's only true love's kiss will wake the sleeping beauty," he said. "Mine is but a token."

He kissed her and she remained asleep.

Bradley didn't understand why he felt such a rush of relief.

"So, how long does the doc say she's going to be sleeping like this?" Sean asked.

Bradley shook his head. "She kind of expected her to already be awake," he said. "If she doesn't wake up by tomorrow, they're going to start running tests."

"Could he have given her an overdose of the drug?" Ian asked.

"That's a possibility," Bradley said. "Or it could be that her system has just been overwhelmed by all she's been through."

Sean moved to the side of the bed and gently pushed some of her hair off her forehead. "You don't think her time here is over?" Sean asked. "You don't think she's done all the good she was meant to do and now God's taking her back?"

"No!" Bradley said. "No. That doesn't make sense. Why now?"

"Well, she came into your life when you were grieving for Jeannine," Ian said. "And now, not only is Jeannine at rest, but you can finally go on with your life."

"Not without Mary," Bradley said. "Not without her."

"Yeah," Sean said, wiping a tear from his eyes. "It was a stupid thought. She's going to be fine. By the way, has Child Services contacted you yet?"

Bradley nodded. "Yeah, they're going to search through their records and send me the information on my daughter. I just have to remember that she's eight years old and has been with a family her whole life. She might not welcome me in her life."

Sean patted Bradley on the shoulder. "It will work out," he said. "And you'll know what to do when the time comes."

"Are you sure you don't want me to go back to Chicago with Sean?" Ian asked. "I feel a little strange living in her house without her being there."

Bradley shook his head. "No, it's good you're there," he said. "Maybe you can keep Mike out of trouble."

Ian chuckled. "Not in this lifetime," he said. "Or the next for that matter."

"Well, I've got to get back," Sean said. "Call me when she wakes up."

"I will, I promise," Bradley said.

"Come on, Ian," Sean said. "I'll give you a ride to Mary's."

The room was once again quiet, except for the sounds of the monitors recording Mary's vital signs. Bradley walked back over to the bed and gazed down at her. Sean's words had brought a fear to his heart that he hadn't experienced in a long time. She couldn't be taken from him. Could she?

He leaned forward and cradled her face in his hand, gently stroking her cheek with his thumb. "You are my heart, Mary O'Reilly," he said. "You can't leave me now. I love you."

He placed a soft kiss on her forehead and then brushed his lips across her cheek.

"Mary, will you marry me?" he whispered.

He placed his lips on hers and kissed her with all the love he had in his heart. A single tear slipped from his cheek and landed softly on hers.

She suddenly took a deep breath and her eyes opened slowly.

"Bradley," she whispered. "What did you say?"

About the author:

Terri Reid lives near Freeport, the home of the Mary O'Reilly Mystery Series, and loves a good ghost story. She lives in a hundred-year-old farmhouse complete with its own ghost. She loves hearing from her readers at author@terrireid.com.

Books by Terri Reid:

Loose Ends – A Mary O'Reilly Paranormal Mystery (Book One)

Good Tidings – A Mary O'Reilly Paranormal Mystery (Book Two)

Never Forgotten – A Mary O'Reilly Paranormal Mystery (Book Three)

Final Call – A Mary O'Reilly Paranormal Mystery (Book Four)

Darkness Exposed – A Mary O'Reilly Paranormal Mystery (Book Five)

Natural Reaction – A Mary O'Reilly Paranormal Mystery (Book Six)

Secret Hollows – A Mary O'Reilly Paranormal Mystery (Book Seven)

Broken Promises – A Mary O'Reilly Paranormal Mystery (Book Eight)

Twisted Paths – A Mary O'Reilly Paranormal Mystery (Book Nine)

Veiled Passages – A Mary O'Reilly Paranormal Mystery (Book Ten)

Bumpy Roads – A Mary O'Reilly Paranormal Mystery (Book Eleven)

The Ghosts Of New Orleans – A Paranormal Research and Containment Division (PRCD) Case File

Made in the USA
Middletown, DE
26 November 2019